LAST CAR
OVER
THE
SAGAMORE
BRIDGE

PETER
ORNER

By the author of
*Love and Shame
and Love*

Praise for PETER ORNER'S
LOVE AND SHAME AND LOVE

"Elegant yet intimate, this is a book that gets into your head and makes itself at home there. Like the James Salter of *Light Years* and *A Sport and a Pastime,* with their acutely observed domestic and sexual tension."
— Maria Russo, *New York Times*

"Like Jeffrey Eugenides's Detroit, Orner's Chicago is microcosm of the twentieth-century European immigrant experience.... Peter Orner has written a magnificent book—magnificent in its unassuming details that nevertheless burst with meaning."
— Lauren Eggert-Crowe, *Los Angeles Review of Books*

"Orner is unusually gifted at creating freighted moments of despair that generate far more impact than their size would suggest." — Ron Charles, *Washington Post*

"An ambitious, kaleidoscopic novel of the Jewish experience in Chicago.... *Love and Shame and Love* serves as an ode not only to the history of Chicago, but to Chicago literature itself."
— Adam Langer, *Chicago Tribune*

"Mr. Orner has found a way of making loss and reclamation exist side by side." — Sam Sacks, *Wall Street Journal*

"In his magnificent second novel, *Love and Shame and Love,* Peter Orner proves he is one of the finest American poets of family weather." — John Freeman, *Toronto Star*

"Beautiful.... Think Saul Bellow (Chicago setting, rollicking Jewish-style comedy) mated with Chekhov (unassuming, devastating detail), set to the twangy thump of early Tom Petty."

—Ted Weesner Jr., *Boston Sunday Globe*

"From his first story collection, *Esther Stories,* on to his most recent novel, *Love and Shame and Love,* Peter Orner has established himself as one of the most distinctive American voices of his generation." —Ted Hodgkinson, *Granta*

"Orner's second novel is a vibrant masterpiece about what it is to live in America — and to live."

—Emily Temple, Flavorpill.com

Praise for
THE SECOND COMING OF MAVALA SHIKONGO

"This novel, about a white American teacher in Namibia, has the same sort of episodic structure, lyrical prose, and completely hypnotic effect as the novels of Michael Ondaatje.... It's a gorgeously written book, very funny, and bursting with soul."

—Dave Eggers, *Guardian*

"Yearning wrapped in gorgeous prose.... If one of literature's jobs is to take the reader to a new experience, this novel richly succeeds." —Robin Vidimos, *Denver Post*

"Orner hits the right notes and no others.... He has written a starvation diary about desire, with as much sexual tension as a bodice-buster. " —Mark Schone, *New York Times Book Review*

"As a work of African provenance, *The Second Coming of Mavala Shikongo* will take its place alongside Saul Bellow's *Henderson the Rain King* and Graham Greene's *The Heart of the Matter*. But it is a book unlike any I have ever read, a miraculous feat of empathy that manages to unearth—in the unlikeliest of spots—the infinite possibilities of the human heart....Orner is incapable of dishonoring his characters. He treats all of them—even the minor figures—with a fierce humanity."

—Steve Almond, *Boston Globe*

"Peter Orner's novel is insightful, believable, unbelievable, funny, and not funny at all....Whether readers know his amazing *Esther Stories* or not, they should run right out and buy *The Second Coming of Mavala Shikongo*." —Ann Beattie

"Quirky, lyrical, comical, full-blown....A gifted short-story writer gives us his first book-length work of fiction, and does so with flair and panache." —Alan Cheuse, *Chicago Tribune*

Praise for
ESTHER STORIES

"Orner doesn't simply bring his characters to life, he gives them souls."

—Margot Livesey, *New York Times Book Review*

"Like Amy Bloom and Charles Baxter, Orner has a gift for revealing how the tragic and the mundane occupy equal berths in our limited mental space."

—John Freeman, *Chicago Tribune*

"The subtle arc of these stories, moving through several years and conflicting points of view, achieves an elegiac tone, even as Orner renders the details of family intimacy with sweet precision."　　　　　　　　　　　—Gail Caldwell, *Boston Globe*

"There's startling intimacy in every story of Peter Orner's debut collection.... Peter Orner is that rare find: a young writer who can inhabit any character, traverse any landscape, and yet never stray from the sound of the human heart."
　　　　　　　　—Judy Doenges, *Washington Post Book World*

"These are stories of unusual delicacy and beauty, and this is a remarkable collection."　　　　　　　　—Charles Baxter

"I was stunned by a sentence or two in every one of the works in *Esther Stories*."　　　　—Rick Moody, *Hartford Courant*

"I consider Peter Orner an essential American writer, one whose stories unfold with a flawless blend of ease and unpredictability."　　　　　　　　　　—Kevin Brockmeier

"A spirit of passionate tenderness broods over these stories. It is as if love, transcending itself, has become a wisdom so perfect it must cherish everything—grace, of course, and awkwardness too, and innocence, and guilt, and haplessness. And yes, clear-sighted and unhonored loss."
　　　　　　　　　　　　　—Marilynne Robinson

"Some of Orner's very short stories are the best of that form that I have read since Isaac Babel's."　　　　—Andre Dubus

LAST CAR

OVER

THE

SAGAMORE

BRIDGE

LAST CAR
OVER
THE
SAGAMORE
BRIDGE

STORIES

PETER
ORNER

LITTLE, BROWN AND COMPANY

NEW YORK   BOSTON   LONDON

Little, Brown and Company
Hachette Book Group
237 Park Avenue, New York, NY 10017
littlebrown.com

First Edition: August 2013

Little, Brown and Company is a division of Hachette Book Group, Inc. The Little, Brown name and logo are trademarks of Hachette Book Group, Inc.

The publisher is not responsible for websites (or their content) that are not owned by the publisher.

The Hachette Speakers Bureau provides a wide range of authors for speaking events. To find out more, go to hachettespeakersbureau.com or call (866) 376-6591.

[CIP tk]

10 9 8 7 6 5 4 3 2 1

RRD-C

Printed in the United States of America

Dedication TK

Hush, Luster said. Looking for them ain't going to do no good, they're gone.

—WILLIAM FAULKNER,

THE SOUND AND THE FURY

CONTENTS

Part I
Survivors

CONTENTS

Part II
The Normal

Part III
In Moscow Everything Will Be Different

CONTENTS

Part IV
Country of Us

PART I
Survivors

FOLEY'S POND

Nate Zamost took that week off school. We wondered what he did those long days other than the funeral, which couldn't have taken more than a few hours. The Zamosts lived in one of those houses just across the fence from Foley's Pond. Nate's sister, Barbara — the family called her Babs — slid under the chain link and waddled down to the water. This was 1979. She was two and a half.

The day Nate Zamost came back to school, we refrained from playing Kill the Guy with the Ball. At recess, we stood around in a ragged circle on the edge of the basketball court and spoke to one another in polite murmurs. We were a group of guys in junior high who hung out together. It's not like we weren't capable of understanding. Some of us even had sisters. Instinctively, we seemed to get it that our role was not to understand, or even console, but, in the spirit of funerals, to act. That being authentically sorry, whatever this might have looked like, would have been out of place, even unwelcome. So we stood there and looked at our shoes and kicked at loose asphalt. Nate went along with it. He played chief mourner by nodding his head slowly. I remember Stu Barkus finally trying to say something.

"Look, it's not like it's your fault," Stu said. "I mean, how could you have known she knew how to slide under the fence?"

Nate looked up from his shoes.

"I taught her."

What could anybody say to that? Barkus took a stab. He'd always been decent like that.

"Well, it's not like you told her to do it when you weren't looking."

"I didn't?"

Barkus had nothing to say anything after that. Nobody else did, either. We let his question hang there. Like Stu Barkus, Nate Zamost was a gentle guy. He was the biggest of us and had a very hard head, but during Kill the Guy with the Ball he'd always go for your ankles and take you down easy. The rest of us were more interested in the raw clawing, the scrum and the mayhem, than in the ball itself. It was the killing-the-guy part. Yet who's to say what goes on behind closed doors between siblings? Nate, like all of us, was thirteen that year. His parents went out for a couple of hours and left him in charge.

Remembering all this now, what comes to me most vividly is my own private anger toward Nate, anger I can still summon. Foley's Pond had always been our secret place and now everybody in town knew all about it. It was wedged inside a small patch of woods, between where Kimball Avenue ended in a stand of bush and trees and the Edens Expressway fence. To the east was the public golf course. Some said the pond wasn't natural at all, that it had been created by runoff from the golf course, that it was nothing but a cesspool of chemicals. Proof of this theory was embodied by the large corrugated drainpipe that hung out over the edge of the pond. Whatever flowed from that pipe wasn't water. Once, Ross Berger dove into Foley's and rose up with green hair and leeches on his thighs. Someone shouted, "It supports life!"

We all stripped to our underwear and jumped in. It was like swimming in crude oil. A fantastic place, Foley's — scragged, infested, overgrown, and gloomed long before Nate Zamost's sister wrecked it. How many mob hits, feet tied to bricks, bobbed and swayed at the bottom of that fetid swamp?

After school we'd retreat to the pond and talk down the waterlogged afternoons. There was nothing beautiful about the place, even in April, except that it was ours. There is something overripe about spring in the Midwest, the wet and green world, the ground itself putrid, rotten, oozing. Foley's was protected by a canopy of trees. The sun crept through only in speckles. Foley's in the rain, the rain smacking the leaves, how hidden we were, talking and talking and talking about God only knows what. Had we been a few years older, we might have drunk beers or smoked joints or brought girls, so they could scream about not wanting to go anywhere near that nasty sludge. It was 1979 and we were thirteen and conspiratorial, and what was said is now out of reach, as it should be.

It took them eleven hours. Foley's was a lot deeper than anybody had thought. The fire department's charts turned out to be inaccurate. Police divers had to come up from Chicago. I think of their rubber outfits, their masks, their flippers, how they waddled along the edge of the pond like big penguins before descending, slowly, into the water. And something else that by now most people may have forgotten and newcomers would have no way of knowing. When they finally did recover her all those hours later, deep in the night, and laid Babs on the grass, Nate's mother refused to acknowledge that the mottle of bloated flesh lit up by high-powered flashlights was her daughter or anybody's. Mrs. Zamost didn't know Foley's. Ross Berger was down there twelve seconds and came up looking like an alien. Mrs. Zamost didn't scream. She wouldn't even touch it. I was there, just outside the ring of lights. She wouldn't even touch it, just shook her head and stepped backward into the dark.

Foley's is a real park now. The Park District manicured it. The trees have been trimmed. There's a wide wood-chip path leading off Kimball Avenue. And they've installed bird feeders, long poles topped with small yellow houses.

OCCIDENTAL HOTEL

He met her at the Occidental in Buffalo, Wyoming. She was a maid at the hotel. She'd come west from Missouri not intending to do much more than stop and work for a few weeks before heading to California. But there was money to be made at the Occidental, especially during conventions. This was February 1912. He'd come for a convention. The state Republican Party was meeting to decide on a successor for McClintock. It was after nine in the morning. She'd knocked on the door twice and waited. Silence. She took the key out of her apron and unlocked the door. A man was sitting on the bed, pulling on a boot. His face was so still it could have been made of wax. His eyes. Even from the door, in the dim light, she could see them, huge and glassy and full of motion. Like small heads bobbing in water.

This one must have checked in late. She held the door.

"Sir?"

"No, come in, come in. I was just, well...Yes. Just. I was just. All right, then."

He pulled on his other boot and, edging his way past without touching her, left the room.

The Occidental wasn't elegant. It was sturdy. The winds of the high plains pounded it, and the hotel stood its ground. On rainy or snowy days, the cherrywood of the walls and all the furniture gave off a sweet, malty smell. She liked the hotel best in the early mornings when the smells—in the thick silence—were more pronounced than the noise. Noise could overpower so many other things.

Two nights later he said he'd leave his wife for her. They were in her small room across the street and down the block from the hotel. He said she'd ransacked his heart the moment she unlocked the door to his room. "You're not a house-keeper," he said. "You're a vandal."

"You looked like you were about to weep," she said.

He laughed. "Politics. I was thinking how we were going to have to settle for Gilhooley if Collins refused to stand. Gilhooley. As if he matters now. Let Gilhooley be King of Prussia!"

Toward dawn he fell asleep. She watched the sun gray, then pink, the frost-crusted window. She saw how dingy and small the room was going to look to him when he awoke. A man with a house and daughters. This wasn't something she ever thought about. Men didn't look at her room. They looked at her, or thought they did. One of his hands lay across her stomach like a plump fish. Moist. The fish rode the rise and fall of her stomach. She wanted it off. She wanted it gone. She had once loved a man in Cape Girardeau, but not enough had come of it. And yet it isn't this man or that man or any man at all. Isn't it the sun leaking through the window again? Isn't it the sun trying to melt this frost? Isn't it this narrow bed and breath dissolving into memory?

SPOKANE

If I tell you something will you listen? Will you not leave and will you listen?

I've listened before.

But will you listen now?

I said yes.

It's another story, Barry.

All right.

Another story story.

I said fine.

It was when I was living in Spokane. I hadn't been there long. Two weeks maybe. I met this guy in a coffee shop.

Right.

Right. Same as always. I liked the book he was reading. We talked about who knows what, and I liked him. I let him take me home and I fucked him. It was gentle, slow. I was new to the city and it was dreary, but I liked the hills and the way the trees grew up out of the sidewalks sideways. Another week with him and I broke my lease and moved into his apartment on the first floor of a little frame house in what people called the even shittier part of Rupert Heights. Because I liked him and it meant saving on rent. My job was decent. I taught art to the second grade at a Montessori school. Liberal, but they only went so far. The pay sucked. His name was Edward. He worked in a B. Dalton in a mall and lived off money his grandfather left him. Maybe he was twenty-four. He said he wanted to go back to school and finish at some point. He had a clarinet in his closet he never played. We lived on a little hump in the street and there was good light in the morning and I set up a darkroom in the bathroom. He didn't mind that I blacked out the little window. For five, six months, I was happy. He was quiet. He could just sit, you know? What I've never been able to train myself to do. Just sit for hours, not bored, not anything. Thinking, I guess. And I thought, I'm smart. I finally made a decent decision in my life and my work is coming along and this Edward with his calmness. Don't laugh at me. He listened to me. I'd tell him everything. About my mother driving all over the lawn and then into the front door, the whole time screaming that we were all foreigners to her, that she didn't know a single soul in our house, that it wasn't even her house. All that shit you've had to hear. And he'd endure it. He never asked questions. His upper lip sometimes quivered, that's all. And you can't know how after talking to myself for so long what it was like to just have this person watch me and listen. I shot him. The pictures are probably still in a box somewhere. And I listened to his stories about his grandfather who worked in a mill, who moved out there from St. Louis to help build the Coulee Dam. He didn't have many friends except for a couple of guys he sometimes played chess with at the coffee shop up the block. Another two or three from the bookstore. He said when he was through reading all the books he wanted to finish, he'd drive to Seattle and make more friends. At night we rented old Bruce Dern movies. I remember one where someone was trying to blow up the Super Bowl. Edward had very timid eyes. He looked away from you when you looked directly at him; he looked away when you kissed him. Fucking him was good and gentle, and when we were through he'd stand by the window wrapped in the top sheet and tell me about his grandfather's prize tomatoes. How his grandpa once took his fattest, spoogiest tomato to the same guy who bronzed baby shoes and said, Immortalize this, why don't you? He never mentioned his parents except once to say they lived in Houston. Another time, though, he told me about a mother who left her kid in the bookstore. The kid was three or four and she wasn't abandoning him or anything—she must have just forgotten she was with him and wandered out of the store without him. The kind of thing every mother probably does once in her life and then has nightmares about for years, but Edward said that what made him remember was that the kid didn't seem to notice. He looked around. Seeing his mother wasn't there anymore, he went on flapping through a car picture book until the mother came back ten minutes later, hysterically shrieking apologies to the kid, to Edward, to everyone standing around. The kid hardly looked up. That night I gripped Edward hard. I tried to love him. From the gut, I tried, and it didn't matter, none of it mattered.

Because one day your Edward, your beautiful Edward of the silence, was gone. And all your dreams were shattered.

I asked if you were going to listen.

It's just that we've been here before. Different guy, different city—What about that guy from Wisconsin? The circus clown?

Trapeze artist. Right, so Edward left. You're right on top of this, Barry. I wasn't there a year. It was December. But because it was his place and he had to come back eventually, I stayed. I promised myself that when he comes back, I'll move out. That I would tell him, Look, we had something for a while, and hey it didn't work out. No hard feelings. You move on. Here's your key and the past-due rent. So long, I told myself I'd tell him. So long. It's amazing how quickly you get used to being left. It's like meeting yourself again. It's not all that lonely. One week went by. No cryptic letter saying it was a great ride but I'm confused. I'm gay. I'm Buddhist and I need to go on a pilgrimage like Siddhartha. I'm scared of love because this one time I got hurt so bad....Nothing. Zero. I went over to the bookstore and the manager said Edward hadn't shown up and hadn't called in. And he was sorry, because he liked him and the customers liked him. Edward was the anchor of the sales team, the guy said. A real future in book selling. I asked at the coffee shop and the people said they hadn't seen him around. Edward's friend with the scarf, the chess mullah, he called himself, said maybe I needed some patience, that maybe I just needed to wait Edward out for a while. When I said I was thinking of going to the police and filing a report or something, this asshole just looks at me and says who am I to say who's missing and who's not. Missing from where? Another week went by. I went to the police and they opened a missing-persons file and said they'd call me if anything turned up. I checked the hospitals — nothing. Meanwhile, I started going out more. To clubs with some other teachers from work. I even dated a social studies teacher a few times, nice guy with a mile-long forehead. The first of the month came around and I didn't pay any rent because I didn't know who to pay it to. I'd given my checks to

Edward for my half. I figured I'd wait until someone called or came around asking. Of course I went through his stuff. Nothing in his papers but some receipts and Visa bills. No family pictures except a bunch of his grandfather leaning against a Buick. So he had no cards from his mother and nobody ever called him? I thought maybe he threw the cards out or his parents didn't know where he was living. Unlike me, he didn't feel the need to blab his history to people who wouldn't want to listen anyway.

What'd this guy look like?

He was bulky, not fat exactly. And he wore it kind of happily, you know? And tall. I think he had more trouble with being tall. He was one of those tall guys who doesn't know what to do with his height. The kind of guy that lanks around and apologies for having to stoop through doorways, except that Edward never apologized, he only sort of waved.

And thus: Shy and gentle! Big and tall! Edward roams. Gone what? Two, three weeks? Rent need not be paid. Sounds like a good deal.

There was a blind guy who lived upstairs.

Now you're just making shit up.

Not totally, but mostly blind. His name was Mr. Ludner. He was easy to forget about. He was so quiet, but some nights Edward would go up there when I was working in the darkroom and sit with him. Mr. Ludner sold televisions at Sears for something like fifty years, and he'd lost his sight gradually, until one morning—this is what he told Edward—he woke up and he couldn't shake out of the blur of his dream. Then he understood he wasn't sleeping. Sometimes—this was the only time you ever heard a peep out of him—he played Mozart arias and tried to sing along in what he thought must have sounded like Italian. Mr. Ludner lived on a small pension and disability. Sears gave him a washer-drier when he retired, which he said was funny since he'd worked in home electronics. And those arias coming from upstairs. Mostly you just forgot about it and then there it was. It's music, and him up there alone, singing alone.

Stace.

You know how I am.

The guy's missing. You're talking about washer-driers.

Right, because for you this would be easy, because for you saying anything is easy.

I'm listening.

Like I said, I was going out with friends more. Finding a life in the hills of Spokane. It's not a bad city, really. You're either from there or you've fled there, and the people who flee there are always somehow a little better off than they are in other places. Spokane takes all comers. People who've failed in Chicago, San Francisco, Denver, Seattle now grace the crumbling sidewalks of a city that's always dying but never pronounced dead —

Stace, please —

He had such gentle fingers. He'd start at my head and run his hand down the length of my body and stop at the bottom of my feet and then just kneel on the floor and stare. And he'd talk to my feet. He'd draw little maps. The Coeur d'Alene River. The old Pacific and Northern Railroad line. The dirty bottoms of my feet, Barry. And I hardly knew him, but I let him look at me in that cold bedroom with one window that only shut on an angle. We plugged the gap with old towels, but it didn't do much good. We slept under mountains of blankets, and I'd wake up in the morning and not want to get out of bed, so I'd walk around with those blankets on my back like I was one big turtle, because it was still so cold.

This isn't right.

And he didn't just talk to Mr. Ludner. Sometimes they played chess, too. And Edward put a bandanna over his eyes and played blindfolded to make the teams fair. They played chess in the dark in Mr. Ludner's little kitchen. So three weeks after Edward left, I finally asked Mr. Ludner if he had any idea. I hadn't wanted to bother him before, upset him. I was standing at the bottom landing and he was coming slowly down the stairs, his long thin cane in front of him, tapping the stairs. Mr. Ludner? I said. Edward's gone. He's been gone almost a month. The old man kept heading toward me down the stairs. When he reached the bottom, he looked at me. Normally he didn't face you when he talked—he talked to you in profile—but that morning he faced me and he said, Yes, that must be true. Three weeks at least. Mr. Ludner straightened his tie. Even though he was retired, he always wore a tie when he left the house. I told him I don't even know if Edward has any family. All I know is that he had a grandfather who died and I'm here in his apartment and I haven't paid any rent. Mr. Ludner laughed when I said that about the rent. Why, my dear, I don't pay any rent, either. Why not? I said, and he laughed again and said, You don't know, do you? Interesting young man Edward. Modest to the teeth. He owns this building, my dear. Passed down to him from the very grandfather you mentioned. His parents are both gone. And he's a good man to let me spend my retirement peanuts on things other than rent. Like fresh fruit, for example. I'm of the opinion that fresh fruit, far more than those vitamin pills they peddle to seniors — But I paid Edward rent, I said. I wrote him checks for my half. Well, he must have mailed the check to himself, Mr. Ludner said. I found out later he never deposited any of my checks. You know how I am about my checkbook. I wouldn't have noticed in a thousand years the money wasn't gone.

All right, now I just want to know.

So this shocked me a little, that he actually owned the house and never said anything, but then I figured he was probably embarrassed. I mean, who at twenty-four owns a house?

Just tell it.

Right, cutting to the chase now, Barry. One night toward the middle of January, Mr. Ludner was playing Mozart when the power went out. It was minus who knows what the fuck with the wind chill. Coldest night of the year and we've got no lights. I opened the inside door and called up to Mr. Ludner, who said the fuse box was in the basement. It was one of those old-fashioned basements with the double doors, you know, that open upward. I asked Edward about the basement once and he said there was nothing down there but mice and rusting bike parts. I crept around the apartment and found a flashlight in the utility drawer. Then I called up to Mr. Ludner and asked him if he had a key No key necessary, he says. The basement doors are always open.

Wait! Say no more! You went down there, and there was Old Edward, Mr. Bohemian Spokane, down in the cellar with his head blown off.

He used a Hefty bag and rubber bands.

Come on.

Not come on.

Stace, I was kidding.

He took pills, but before that, he wrapped himself up in garbage bags because he didn't want us to smell him. And we didn't, because of the plastic and because of the cold. Mr. Ludner said it was probably because he wanted to die in his grandfather's house, the house his grandfather left him, but that he also wanted us to go on living there because he was a good man. Mr. Ludner said Edward was a good man. When I found him, there were these black bugs, the kind that live straight through winter, the kind that sort of hop backward, crawling all over the plastic. He was still wearing shoes. But let me back it up, Barry. Let me take it step by step. I went around back to the basement doors and brushed away a crust of old snow, pulled them open, and went down the wooden stairs. I found the fuse box on the far right wall, where Mr. Ludner said it would be, and flicked the switch. I heard Mr. Ludner shout out the window, Hurrah! Mozart came back on. Then I found a string for the light and pulled. Not much there. Like Edward had said. Some cardboard boxes. A pair of old ski poles. A tire. A stack of waterlogged phone books. And then right beside the furnace, I saw a mattress with some books on it. A dirty yellow pillow. Some socks. And a bag of Cheetos. Edward thought it was funny that he still loved Cheetos. The crunchy ones, not the puffy. He said he hated the way the puffy ones melted in your mouth before you even had a chance to chew. And I thought, Holy shit, he lives down here. But for some reason, I wasn't really freaked out. I just whispered, *Edward? Edward?* Jesus, Edward, why are you living down here when you've got a nice apartment upstairs? When it's your house? I'll move out and you can have your place back, but for godsakes, don't live down here. And I'm talking to the walls of the basement as if he can hear me, as if he's hiding in the dark corners and watching me. Isn't that nuts?

I love you. You've got to know I love you, honey, I—

So I walk around whispering to him, thinking he's either hiding or he'll be back soon and I'll wait for him and tell him, Look, I'll leave. I'll find a new place—

Shhhhhhhhh. It's all right. Enough.

Lumped against the far wall like an old sack of leaves. And you want to know what my first thought was? Totally ridiculous. That it was a bag of clothes somebody had meant to drop off at the Goodwill and never got around to—I thought maybe I'd rummage through and find a good pair of Levi's. Least Edward could do was leave me a good pair of Levi's before I went my merry way. Then I stepped closer, and it couldn't have been more obvious what it was. And I started to smell him, even though he was half frozen. But it's strange. I wanted to touch him. I wasn't terrified and I didn't scream when I felt the squish of decay. Like this was all very fucking normal. Like this was the way some people lived and died, and this was the way other people found out about it. Like I wasn't surprised. And I knew—without knowing why or how—that he'd done this to himself. Edward in late morning, on the stoop. Edward sitting on the sidewalk with a long piece of grass in his mouth. Edward naked, kneeling. Edward in a wool hat with a tassel. Edward holding a bronze tomato, early evening. Edward eating cereal with a fork. Edward wrapped in plastic bags and rubber bands. And I'm still calm and I just walk right out of there and up the stairs and go to Mr. Ludner's and knock on his door and go into the dark of his apartment with his Mozart and tell him Edward's dead in the basement. I'm pretty sure Edward's dead in the basement. And he stood up, said quietly, Would you wait a moment? Would you sit down and wait a moment? Then he picked up his cane by the door and went down the stairs. Tap, tap, tap, down the stairs slowly. I listened to him, listened to each step. And Mr. Ludner found him down there, somehow, and ripped the bag open and felt his face, Edward's decomposing face. Then he left him and came back up the stairs. He called to me from the landing. Miss Mueller, he said, looks like our boy didn't want to trouble us. Then Mr. Ludner gagged. I sat there in the dark with that music on the stereo and listened to the old man retch. The coroner said it'd been at least ten days.

Stace.

He was living down there, Barry, reading, and when he couldn't even do that anymore —

Stace.

Don't touch me.

Stace.

I said don't touch me.

THE POET

Since his stroke, the old poet hadn't been able to read his poems, much less write any new ones. Still, those few summers he had left, they trotted him out, a novelty act, and stood him up at the podium. He'd stare forward, eyes wide, clearing his throat. His redheaded lover would hold him by the elbow and he'd do the best he could, retrieving half-remembered phrases out of the dark muddle of his brain, and the crowd, not knowing much more about him other than that here before them is what's left of an important poet, would watch with reverence, even awe, and then, finally, fear.

He asked: *Why can't our dreams be content with the terrible facts?*

HERB AND ROSALIE SWANSON AT THE COCOANUT GROVE

Two decades later Herb Swanson began to tell the story at dinner parties. He knew every inch of the trivia. He knew that the forgotten movie star who burned to death that night was named Buck Jones. Nowadays people don't know the guy from Adam, Herb would say, but back then Buck Jones, no joke, was big as Gene Autry. Herb knew that the final death toll was 492, including the five firemen, not 474 like some accounts still claim. Herb knew that the name of the busboy who struck the match that accidentally lit the ceiling and started the greatest conflagration in the history of Boston — to this day you can't call a business Cocoanut Grove within Boston city limits, not even if you sell coconuts — was named Stanley Tomaszewski. Wretched Stanley Tomaszewski. He'd been trying to change a light bulb. He needed light to see better and so lit a match. The ceiling caught. Tomaszewski escaped out the kitchen door and lived the rest of his life guilt-struck in Waltham, hearing those screams in his sleep.

Then Herb would lower his voice and say in a whisper coated with breathy awe: Listen, it's just after ten. Ro and I are upstairs in the dining room. Micky Alpert's just launched into the first chords of the "Star-Spangled Banner." There are palm trees and piña coladas all over the place, like we're in Tahiti. Waiters spin through the crowd with trays hoisted over their heads like ancient high priests sending up offerings to the gods when it—

When it—

Herb would always hustle past the actual fire part. What mattered when Herb told his Cocoanut Grove story was the great aftermath. The courage of the firemen, the heroics of the policemen, the essential contributions of the Women's Army Relief Corps. How the people of Boston, Massachusetts, joined together in the face of such disaster, a beautiful thing amid all that incalculable horror. It even prepared people, Herb said, for what was to come soon enough with our boys being sent home from France wrapped in the flag.

Still, Herb couldn't completely ignore the fire itself. His credibility depended on it. The almighty fact of his and Rosalie having been there, having survived it. Got lucky was all he'd really say. Our number wasn't up. All there is to it. Our table was near one of the few exits that didn't get blocked up with people right away. We were the fourth couple out the door. For years Rosalie never said anything when Herb told the story, and this, too, gave it a mystique. It was too painful for her to talk about, to remember. Yet at some point, when both of them were well into their sixties, as Herb continued to rattle on and on about flammable ceiling material, how the biggest problem from a fire-safety perspective was that the few exit doors opened inward, how there were no sprinklers either, how four brothers from the little hamlet of Wilmington, Massachusetts, all died in it and the town put up a statue of them on the green — Rosalie began to enter the story with her own details, quietly at first. She'd talk about how the fire was less like a wall and more like a flapping curtain. She'd talk about its not being hot either, but windy. She'd talk about the soot-covered sailor in the famous *Life* photograph, an unconscious barefoot girl draped across his arms like a bride, the sailor all the newspapers called an angel dispatched from heaven. Well, yes, I did see him that night. *Before it.* A hard man not to notice — let me be honest. But I wasn't a slouch then, either. I swished by him in my latest red dress. I was thin then, if you can believe it. Still hippy, but thin, maybe even a little uniquely pretty in a certain light, and yes, sailor boy winked at me. And Herb would shout across the table (because even then it was a performance and they were still in cahoots): Everything she says is true. Unique? Of course! Beautiful! Beautiful then, beautiful now, my Rosie. I wanted to break the jack tar's neck, but Rosie said, *Let him stare, it's patriotic.*

And Rosalie, whispering now: *After he left that girl on the sidewalk, that sailor went back inside.*

And Herb: *Poor kid. Died of his burns two days later at Boston City.*

Herb Swanson was a dentist, everybody's favorite dentist. In his line, he needed a reputation for telling a decent story. Rosalie didn't need stories any more than she needed these interminable dinner parties Herb loved so much. Yet there was something, wasn't there, even for her, about that fire? Maybe it was that sailor's famous, cockeyed, confident face. An unshaped face, an unravaged face. In any case, something happened when Rosalie joined Herb's story. It was as if she'd actually known it.

As if that dead boy was more to her than just a picture she'd seen so many years ago in a magazine. Because none of it was ever true. The Cocoanut Grove didn't happen to them. She never saw that sailor, before or after, and neither had Herb. There was no "Star-Spangled Banner," at least not in their ears. (Herb read that somewhere; Herb read everything somewhere.) As for the sober facts: They were at that club that night. This much was whole truth. But Herb's stomach was acting up, and this time it was more than a bad case of gas. They left an hour before the fire. Saved by indigestion! But what kind of story would that make? A one-shot laugher, not the kind you tell and tell again. And far beyond this, it was not the kind of story that gave you the incontestable authority of the messenger. Anyway, twenty, thirty, forty years on, who was going to know or care? Harmless table talk. And if you think about it, in a way, they had escaped, hadn't they? They just didn't know that's what they were doing when they retrieved their coats from the hatcheck sweetie (she didn't survive—she was from Malden, engaged, one of the last bodies recovered) and marched out into the chill and *brr* of an ordinary Boston November night. Why split hairs? Escaping's escaping.

Rosalie began to play along more intensely. Her eyes would get bleary. She'd talk with her fork suspended near her mouth, as if something crucial to understanding everything had only then just crossed her mind. Everybody would stop chewing to listen. Like a horde except that nobody was moving in the same direction. You see? Had people moved in the same direction, maybe it would have been different. See? What you have to understand is that it wasn't the heat or the flames or even the dread smoke, it was how the people—

Then she'd pause and take a breath, her fork still up in the air by her ear: I'm not saying I blame them. No. God, no. I love them. How can you not love them?

Somehow her saying this was worse than the melting walls and the charred bodies and the unopenable doors, or even the useless, desperate screams, which she never talked about but were always there in her voice. Herb knew how many fire departments responded to the alarm, trucks as far as New Bedford roared to Boston. Herb knew the score of the Boston College–Holy Cross game. B.C. 12, Holy Cross 55. He knew how many young and virile lives were saved by that humiliation, because Boston College called off the victory party scheduled for that night in the Grove's Melody Lounge. He knew the name of the last Buck Jones picture, *Forbidden Trail,* where Buck, playing a cowhand, not only saves Mary and her mother from the villain Mr. Coffin, he also rescues a man from a burning cabin. All this before being unjustly accused of arson and murder himself! But Herb Swanson had no talent for putting people inside that club, really inside, and the truth is that he began to be a little frightened by his wife. The last thing Rosalie cared about was hoodwinking anybody about what she did or didn't see that night in 1942, and yet when she got started in about things like fingernails tearing the flesh of the shoulders, it was as though she couldn't stop. *I don't blame them, I really don't. Clawing each other. Even husbands and wives.* And Herb would watch her anxiously, fidgeting, waiting for an opening and a chance to recapture the story. Bring it back to the busboy, Stanley Tomaszewski, and an interview he did with the *Globe* on the thirtieth anniversary of the fire, in 1972, where he said he prays for the souls of those innocents every day and often visits their graves, the ones that are here in Massachusetts. He told the reporter that the movie star was buried too far away, but that he'd always wanted to make that trip out to California. There's your human interest! Stanley Tomaszewski guilty and prostrate before the headstones! Because it was almost as though Rosalie (even though she always denied it) judged people for trying to save themselves, which was wrong and terrible and not at all the point. The point was glory. The point was redemption. Think of all the good that came out of that fire. Municipal solidarity. Nationwide sympathy and understanding. New fire codes for every public building in the United States of America. Pivotal advancements in emergency medicine and response...

And there's a night, isn't there, when Rosalie stares at Herb as if there's nobody else in the room, even though they are having dinner with the Selvins and Tony Bickleman and his latest wife, Maureen, and they're all sitting right there. Not their fault, such rage, Rosalie says, not their fault. There's nobody else in the room, and Herb watches her watching him, and he tries not to listen, and he vows to himself he'll never bring up the goddamn Cocoanut Grove again, ever. He even goes one further and promises himself that one of these days he'll come clean, which after these years would make a good story in itself. It never happened, folks. We weren't there. I lied. My dear friends, let me be frank, the long and the short of it was (pause, drumroll) Pepto-Bismol. I stand before you a prevaricator. And he can hear Harvey Selvin saying, For Christ's sake, Herb, it's a story. And Tony Bickleman: And I wasn't shot at Anzio either, shot at, but not shot. I always say shot. What's the difference? Coulda bin, couldn't I a bin?

Around the middle of the 1980s, not long after he retired, Herb did stop telling the story, at least in public. And when he stopped, Rosalie stopped. She'd never initiated the story; she only carried it places it wasn't supposed to go. Herb in his chair in the den looking out at the backyard and Rosalie on the patio reading, slowly turning pages, or not turning pages at all, the woman could spent five minutes on the same page, and still the ceiling ignites and the flames spread across the walls and he tries to run and can't. Herb flings himself against the crowd, elbows cocked like an offensive lineman, trying to use his bulk to plow forward, shouting absurdly, "Make way! I'm a doctor!" While Rosalie remains behind, at their table. Rosalie sips her Scotch. She crosses and recrosses her legs. She rubs the clean white tablecloth with her palm. After he stopped telling the Cocoanut Grove out loud, this is the part that was most alarming. This is what made Herb try to free his brain from those two words the way the city of Boston banished them from the commercial register. Rosalie serene while he and everyone else in the place—

When she died, it all got more vivid. The specter of her sitting and watching. She left the same way. That morning she'd been talking about craving fresh cucumber salad. *When was the last time I had cucumber salad? At my Aunt Gert's in the fifties?* As she napped in the guest room with her clothes on, a stroke took her away, on a Monday afternoon. It wasn't that he hadn't known her. He had. It wasn't that she hadn't loved him. She had, in her way. And she'd always been Rosie, always the girl in the red dress who got the twice-over from sailors and sauced it right back. Still, she always held herself, not alone, apart. Maybe this was why people craved her sole attention. When the kids were little and even after they'd gone away, they were still always trying to get their mother away from Herb in order to be listened to, beg advice, confess. They didn't want Herb's bigheartedness, his hugs, his compassion. *Mom, I shoplifted. Mom, I'm strung out. Mom, I'm getting a divorce. Mom, I'm broke again. Mom, I'm tired, I can't figure out why I'm so tired all the time.* And she'd stare back at them as if they were strangers. No answers or empathy or even comfort. But something. What did you give—what? Tell me. Talk to me, Ro, I'll listen. Herb in his chair by the window, overlooking her azaleas. The glare of the sun white now against the glass. A frenzied waiter douses a blazing tinsel palm tree with seltzer water, and Rosalie laughs, raises a long, thin finger slowly to her lips, and breathes, Let it come, Herb, just let it—

*M*y old boss E.J. once told me he was famous for goofy hats. This was when he worked the lock-in ward at Hennepin County. The hats, E.J. said, came to represent his solidarity with the ones called patients. One day he'd wear a sombrero, the next a feathered Tyrolean, the day after that a plastic hard hat with placeholders for two beers they gave away free at a Twins game. He said they began to trust him and treat him as if he were one of them, which meant they toned down the loony and just talked to him the way they talked among themselves, which was like everybody else in the world talks to everybody else in the world, normal with a touch of nuts. E.J. told me this as he lay in a bed at Nicollett Methodist. How that job on the psych ward was less about the daily incidents of mayhem, which he could recall vividly, than a sense of camaraderie he'd never felt before or since. Looking back, he wondered whether he hadn't been most alive, most in tune with his fellow men, those years he worked the lock-in. They trusted me, E.J. said. They had nothing left to lose. This was when he could talk, because in the weeks and days before he died, he stopped talking altogether and only screamed if you went near him. The nurses needed two orderlies to hold him down to give him his shots. Last I spoke to him was on the phone. I put the receiver down on the table and just listened to him scream.

MINNEAPOLIS, 1984

AT THE KITCHEN TABLE

The lady officer told her if she wanted a family burial she'd have to make special arrangements for him to be retrieved. The state will assume all burial costs if this isn't the case, but in such case he can't be buried anywhere but in the Department of Corrections' own plot in Murfreesboro. In whichever case, she, Mrs. Alper, the lady officer said, was required to come up to Caledonia tomorrow morning to sign identification papers and to collect personal items such as are wanted. The rest will be properly disposed of. But please, Mrs. Alper, understand, if you wish to take your son's body home, you must be accompanied by a licensed mortician and a funeral services vehicle. Then she said in a lower, different voice, a voice that nearly recognized the notion of sorrow: You can't take him home in your own car is what I'm saying is D.O.C. policy.

Mrs. Alper? Mrs. Alper?

Jean Alper at the kitchen table, Gastonia, North Carolina. September 1986. Tomorrow is tomorrow. The phone is on the floor. It's ceased to repeat itself. There may be other sounds out the open kitchen window, but she doesn't hear them. Someone might be mowing a lawn. She wouldn't know. It's still today and he's lying on his back someplace they keep cold. It's cold where they've got him, and she imagines a large walk-in refrigerator stacked tall with frozen breaded chicken patties and white plastic buckets of soup, frost growing up his fingernails, across his eyelids. She wants to laugh. It's June. So cold. She tired, Lord, did she tire. Maybe she could have tried harder, but with Aubrey dead and her brothers so far away and her working nine, ten hours a day, it was hard. She could have moved them away from here, but where? Charlotte? She didn't know anybody in Charlotte. She knew hardly anybody in Gastonia anymore. Anyway, some years you had to sit tight with what you had. She's got a job. A job's a job. Well, I can make excuses till kingdom come and they won't call an undertaker or iron a decent dress by 5:30 tomorrow morning. At least three hours to Murfreesboro, and shouldn't she be there by nine? He did what he wanted, stubborn as his father, but Aubrey, when it came down to it, was all bluster. Knock the man over with your finger. Jordy, though, never afraid of anything or anybody. Since he was three and tearing up the carpet, her tomato plants, hair of neighbors' daughters. The neighbors called him Pixie Terror until he got so big so fast he was just Terror. Then they didn't call him anything. Her fingers thump the table in the silence. So cold. It isn't as if she doesn't have people to call. Vince in Wilmington and Dave and Julia in St. Louis. It's how to say it. Who'd believe it? That it was only simple fear. Jordy? Man the size of a small office building. Because inside there something happened. Supposed to, right? Supposed to change you, right? On visiting days she'd say, What, baby, what? Him sitting there fiddling with his shirt like it had a button, but there were no buttons. They hurting you? Somebody touching you? And him shaking his head, not that, and waving her away and coughing and laughing and saying, *Stupid enough to end up here, stupid enough to be rattled by the doors locking.* And when she drove home that day, she thought she understood. So easy. Funny almost, doors. As if he expected there not to be any.

The way he said it, like doors existed independent of what he was doing in there, and yet she understood. There's doors and there's doors. Once, another day, he'd rammed his head against the wall in that little ferociously lit room like she wasn't there at all, kept doing it and doing it and doing it, until the guard came and pulled her away, his forehead gashed and pouring. It wasn't a steady descent to wherever the fear was taking him; it was slow, and some visiting days it wouldn't be there at all. Some days he let her touch him, his body falling so heavily into hers he'd almost knock her over. A few of the guards were kind to her. They sometimes looked at her as if she were a vision of their own mother driving four hours to be humiliated, to be searched, to have the insides of her thighs patted down for the love of a son who didn't deserve it. Lots of guys had to talk to their visitors through the glass, but for Jordy Alper's mother they unlocked the lawyers' room, and Jordy would say, All right, Ma, in here you have to talk like a lawyer. How's my appeal going? And she'd say all she could think of to say, which was I've been filing motions galore for you, honey, and it's all a wait-and-see, and sometimes his hands would grip the table in order to talk and he'd say things he never said in his life, like Tell me about you, Ma, talk about you, and she'd try and he'd listen, clutching the edge of the table. Mostly he stopped shaving, but some days she'd get there and he'd be clean-shaven and this made it worse, not because he was so pale and bleeding at the chin but because he'd want so much out of it. He'd force himself to laugh hard and long at her stories and smile with his face when he talked, and watching him perform would exhaust her, and he'd read this exhaustion in her eyes and stand up and call the guard and say, *Let her go home.* No, who'd believe it? My God, so cold. But hadn't anybody ever noticed that even after he sprouted up taller than his uncles, he still slouched into rooms like he was apologizing for something? Because people turned from the boy. They always had. She's making excuses. He was a chubby baby with fat, grippable elbows. He never cried, only yelped sometimes, and some nights Aubrey couldn't stand to be near his own son, because he said the baby looked at him with eyes that weren't a baby's. Sorrow's years different from sadness. Maybe she's always known this. She looks at the table. There's a small plate with a half-eaten piece of toast. She doesn't remember it. Sadness, always lots of it, but this is something new and will become part of her in a way Aubrey's absence never has. The call a shock and nothing at all like a shock. Sitting right here, the phone rings, the lady officer says words, and all of it the start of something she always knew she'd be.

Your husband dies, you're a widow. There's not even a word for what I am now. Jordy, my only only. Why not scream it? She sits, motionless now, already hating two tongue waggers from work, Brenda and Denise. (You hear it? About Jean's son? Awful, just terrible, but that boy was bad bad news. Made holy terror look like Donny Osmond.) Funny, isn't it? Hilarious — and then they talk about you at the Coke machine.

Early summer, just after nine in the morning. The window's open. The curtain bloats, settles, bloats, settles. Jean Alper's feet are flat on the floor. It will be a long time before the crickets shriek. She'll wait right here.

GRAND PACIFIC HOTEL,
CHICAGO, 1875

One hotel maid said her screeching resembled the sound of a peacock. Far more horrifying was Mrs. Lincoln's silence. Late at night she would dress and roam the shoe-lined corridors of the hotel as if she were searching for something in all those hallways that looked identical to everyone but her. It was those shoes. All those shoes waiting to be shined like the ghosts of so many feet.

And the corridors themselves seemed to change every time she wandered down them. There were nights, early mornings, when she couldn't find her way back to her room. Even she changed—moment by moment—and this is why there are no safe harbors anywhere. Even our own bodies betray us, every moment of every day. Even you people who understand nothing must understand this. Don't you see? Motion is where the loss is. If we could only be still. But then how to search? How to find?

She leaves his side of the bed open. The people think he never slept. They think he stood vigil all night long. If they knew. He slept hard, with his mouth open. I am the one who did not sleep.

RAILROAD MEN'S HOME

Henry's enemy lived in the room next door. Sometimes I saw him in the hall carrying his portable television. That TV was cradled in his arm the day I shouted, I need help, Henry's fallen down. The man walked calmly into Henry's room and set the TV down on the floor. Then he knelt and checked Henry's pulse at the neck, professionally, using two fingers.

"Poor sap," he said. "He thought I'd go before him."

"There's no hope?"

"Someone should alert Sister Harris. She'll want to get the room ready for the next contestant. This is prime real estate. Two windows. Most of us only have one. Can you imagine?"

"Would it be all right if I had a little time?" I said.

"Of course, they'll want to fumigate it first."

"A few minutes, only to—"

"Who are you, anyway? A grandson? Nephew hoping for an inheritance? Pennies under the mattress? Don't kid yourself."

"I'm one of the listeners."

"Listeners are supposed to spread the visits around."

"I know."

"You don't think the rest of us aren't about ready to croak? He had you convinced he was the only one?"

Together, we lifted Henry off the floor. It was surprising how light he was. We hoisted too quickly. Like when you brace yourself to raise a log that turns out to be hollow. We set Henry gently on the bed. His enemy yanked off his tennis shoes without untying the laces. He studied Henry in his clean white tube socks. Henry was fastidious. He shaved twice a day, once in the morning and once, he said, at teatime. His enemy was on the fat side and had small, sharp teeth like a ferret's.

"You hated him back?" I said.

The man snorted and sat down on the one chair in the room. "No. My enemy is Vern in East Wing."

I laughed.

"I'm meaning this sincerely." He spoke to the corpse. "How about a truce, Henry? Okay? Bygones be all gones?"

"You tortured him with the TV."

"Look, I'm hard of hearing. For years I invited him over for Johnny Carson. And Tom Snyder's show. He would have liked Tom Snyder. Snyder's an intellectual, just like—"

"He said you could hear your TV in Milwaukee. He said you took a shower with it."

"Now these are exaggerations."

Henry's last words to me, only a few minutes before all this, were "I tire of you." It wasn't the first time he put it that way. I'd always worried that my too-open eyes and never knowing what to say were literally boring Henry to death. Now I'd done it, I'd murdered him. His enemy looked like he was about to doze off, the TV nuzzled against his chest like a baby. I walked over to the bulletin board and looked at the new Goya picture.

I would check out art books for Henry from the library. He'd rip out the color plates and tack them up. Goya was his favorite. Henry claimed Goya was one of the few artists who truly understood the nature of everyday degradation. Cervantes, too. Look to the Spanish. They've been shat on enough to understand. This latest Goya was a drawing of a man hanging by the neck from a branch. A woman standing on the ground below him was reaching up into the man's mouth.

"His teeth," Henry had said. "See how it ends? Napoleon's dragoons rape and pillage. You get strung up. All is quiet. After that, some crone sneaks up and rips off your dentures."

I looked at the dangling man, his baggy pants, his sad feet. What good were his teeth now?

My job was to listen, but often Henry would demand that I talk. About what? Anything, he'd say. Just talk. I told him the truth about anything I could think of. About not being sorry my dog ran away, about my lack of friends. I told him the last thing I wanted to do after school was go home. He took no pity on me, which is probably why I kept showing up. Sometimes he'd hold up his hand and in this way demand silence. It was in those moments we might have known each other best, and even appreciated each other's company.

Once, Henry said, "You know what?"

"What?"

"You end up living someone else's life."

"Really?"

"One day you won't recognize yourself in the mirror. I guarantee it. One day you'll wake up and your face—alien territory."

"Whose did you want to live?"

"Don't you listen?"

I opened one of Henry's windows. Rain was falling now in invisible streaks. You had to squint to see it. It's strange to look at a street you know so well from a different angle. Here was a street I'd grown up on, walked up and down my whole life. I could never get used to the view from up there. It wasn't the place I knew. The wet September street, the empty sidewalk, the few cars passing, and the sounds they made, rain quishing beneath tires. It's so simple, I thought, even I could figure it out. St. Johns Avenue goes on without you.

Henry lying on his bed. His enemy tsking, gloating. I asked him again, would he mind giving me a little more time? Alone?

He stood. "You have nine hours until rigor mortis."

"He was an intellectual," I said.

The man nodded and, with his TV, did a little shuffle of a dance out of the room.

Not a shred of the old building remains. Where it once stood, there are three new houses, basketball hoops in the empty driveways. It was an old-age home for retired employees of the Chicago and Northwestern Railroad. Such places used to exist around Chicago. The home looked like a kind of Greek temple, with a set of huge pillars in front. To walk those steps was like going somewhere. But at the same time vines crawled all over the front, as if even then the building knew it didn't belong in the neighborhood and was trying to camouflage itself. People seemed to notice it only after they started to tear it down. Before the railroad bought the place, sometime in the twenties, it had been a convent. When it changed over, some of the old nuns stayed on to care for the railroad men. Henry used to wonder out loud where all the young nuns went, if there were ever any young nuns. He said he sometimes roamed the halls looking for virgin ghosts to violate. He never once mentioned trains. He'd been a conductor on the Chicago/Kenosha line for fifty-odd years. I visited him on Tuesdays, sometimes Thursdays.

I sat on the edge of the bed. Henry's eyes were still open. If I was insignificant before, what was I now? His enemy poked his head back in.

"A cavalry of habits is on the way. Someone else must have heard you yelling and pressed a button. God forbid anybody gets out of bed."

"All right," I said.

"What'd you do? Drugs?"

"Stole."

"How many hours?"

"Hundred."

"What are you up to?"

"Passed it. Court signed off."

"Ah, a saint."

He stepped toward the bed and grabbed hold of one of Henry's big toes. I made a move to stop him, but seeing it was done out of some kind of affection, I let it go.

PLAZA REVOLUCIÓN,
MEXICO CITY, 6 A.M.

A woman who sells television antennas in the Zócalo walks slowly through a mostly empty plaza as the sun begins to rise and thinks of her sister who lives in Ohio now. Her sister who was beautiful before she had children. Teresa never had children herself. But nobody called her beautiful to begin with. She and Reuben tried for years. Why all this again now? The light, something about the changing light. As if a sheet were slowly being lifted off the face of the earth. She crosses the plaza and thinks of a sleeping face, some lost morning. Her sister's name is Rosella, a name Rosella always said she hated though it went so well with her beauty. She's not lost, she's in a place called Dayton.

The light slants across the plaza, slightly pinkish now. The four-sided arch looms. It's really an unfinished building they call an arch. They started to build a new parliament here, but the land was too marshy, and so they had to stop. Didn't they take off your shoes before they started to build? Maybe politicians who build parliaments never take off their shoes. But aren't all buildings, like people, unfinished? We build and we build and still we're not done? I know where to find Rosella and still she's gone? It's a question for God, who looms above this arch as indifferent to sisters as he is to parliaments, as he seems to be about so many other things. When they were girls, Rosella once slammed her on the nose with a teapot. Teresa forgave her sister the same afternoon. She forgives her again this morning. For the teapot. For not being beautiful anymore. For being so far away she might as well not exist. Rosella. From her eyes not from her mouth in the now noisier morning.

HORACE AND JOSEPHINE

My aunt Josephine would slip fifty-dollar bills into the front shirt pocket of my brother's Cub Scouts uniform. Go and buy yourself something nice for a damsel, soldier. Then she'd put one of her long, exquisite fingers to her lips to let my brother know that her secret of General Grant should stay between them. And even after Uncle Horace was completely disgraced and they were living in Aunt Molly's spare room, Aunt Josephine still did that with the fifties. Because she walked around Aunt Molly's cramped little stucco house on Wampanoag Street the same way she did her marble-floored palace way up at the top of the hill on President Avenue. The fact that Horace had gone pauper didn't change her. Or the paintings that now hung on Aunt Molly's walls, the paintings Josephine had hid for months in my grandmother's attic in order to save them from the public auction.

To Josephine, the paintings, one of which she claimed was an early Matisse (a whispy nude), represented who she was, not who she once was. True, they no longer adorned a grand front hall like the one she used to hustle guests through with a flurry of wild waving: Don't dawdle, come in, come in! Come in! Yet even at Molly's, where the facts of what had happened to them could not have been starker, Aunt Josephine's eyes gave nothing away. Not regret, never anger. Uncle Horace had a similar take. His spectacular plunge from the upper stratosphere of Fall River society didn't stop him from hectoring anyone who came near him about the glories of high finance. That he'd been brought so low was proof that he'd been a true gambler, the sort of visionary American who built this country. You think John D. Rockefeller didn't take any risks with other people's money?

By the mid-seventies it was well known throughout southeastern Massachusetts and all of Rhode Island — even the *Providence Journal* got into the act and put it on the front page — that Horace's sham investment scheme, his robbing of Peter to pay Paul, as my mother put it years later, had bankrupted not only him, but nearly took the rest of the family — and much of Jewish Fall River — down as well. After decades of Horace paying 8 or 9 percent monthly interest, all his investors lost their principal when the whole thing went bust. They say nobody in the family came out unscathed when it came down to the accounting, except, as my grandmother used to mutter under her breath, Aunt Pauline's husband, Ira, because Ira Pinkus, the lousy foot dragger, had never earned an honest dollar to begin with and knew a con when he saw one.

Horace and Josephine were our family's famous once-hads. Horace Ginsburg was still the son of an upholsterer who'd taken his father's tailor shop and built an investment corporation with subsidiaries in five states. We used to make clothes, now all we make is money. So what if it was all a snow job, a

paper swindle, and that when it came time to do the accounting the man owed millions to creditors? A man of business is
measured in this world by what it looks like he's, forget about
the actualities. And for years, in addition to the house on Highland Avenue, Horace and Josephine did, it seemed, have a
Manhattan condo on East Seventy-Seventh *and* a beach house
on the Cape at Dennis *and* a pied-à-terre in Nassau. What about
his front-row season tickets to Harvard football? Horace didn't
go to Harvard. But what's it matter, he used to sing, if Harvard's not my alma matter? I give them wads, wads….Once,
Uncle Horace said to my brother, You know what the secret of
philanthropy is? Never give a single dime to anybody who
needs it. And, of course, he had Josephine Sharkansky, the
most exquisite and cosmopolitan girl of Hebrew extraction
ever to grace the muddy banks of the Taunton River. They had
it all, so it's no wonder people shoveled their money at Horace.
People wanted to know the things that Horace and Josephine
talked about, modern art, Carl Jung, Nehru; travel to the places
they traveled to, Saint-Tropez, Copenhagen, Nairobi. Everyone, even my never stylish, always frumpled grandparents,
wanted a piece of that action.

Even after it was all out in the open, Horace and Josephine
held tight to their mystique by tossing an enormous costume
ball in the waning days before the auction. If we're going to
fail, Josephine must have told Horace, let's do it grandly, loudly,
with abandon, my puckery darling. Horace went as a conquis-
tador; Josephine as Golda Meir, who, she noted, was a librarian
before she became a prime minister. We lunched with her in
Tel Aviv. Extraordinary woman, marvelous sense of irony…

I came along a lot later. Long after Horace and Josephine's

glory days had been reduced to stacks of overexposed photographs stuffed in envelopes and pushed to the back of lower desk drawers lined with tissue-thin white paper. By the time I was old enough to know what was going on, the family's standard of living had long since plummeted, and the house on the Cape at Yarmouth was a sun-glared, overexposed memory. There were other disasters: The state built an interstate smack through my grandfather's furniture store; Uncle Charlie's cookie business went belly-up because of the price of sugar, something to do with a coup d'état in the Dominican Republic. In the late seventies, my humbled relatives summered in the Fall River swelt.

But as a nine-year-old so shy I only stared at the stains in Aunt Molly's carpet, even I understood there was something different about visiting this house. When we visited Horace and Josephine, we were treated like visiting dignitaries, midget princes from the far-off Midwest. On a visit to Fall River in the summer of 1976, Josephine greeted us in front of Molly's squeaky screen door and announced: "Nephews, I've made pâté." We settled in the small front room crowded with furniture and sipped tea. I'm sure it was the first time in my life I had ever used a saucer. Aunt Josephine conversed with us. Her sisters, Molly and my grandmother, didn't so much talk as force-feed. Plates of brownies would materialize, one after the other, as though they'd been baking nonstop for months. Josephine crossed her legs and asked what we thought of Andy Warhol. Didn't we think his significance somewhat overstated? After stammering and sipping our tea, we were released to Horace, who was waiting in that spare bedroom with his pipe. We took turns kissing his fuzzled face. He was sitting in the only chair. He motioned us to sit on the bed. A gnarled man, he seemed to shrink every summer. He stood, clapped his hands, and sputtered smoke into my brother's face.

"A peanut-butter salesman?" he shouted. "Truman hawked hats, but haberdashery is at least a profession."

"Jimmy Carter is a businessman farmer," my brother intoned, brushing hair out of his eyes. " His peanut operation is a major agricultural concern. He also served his country aboard a nuclear submarine. He's been governor of the thirty-first largest state. He knows what he's doing, frankly—injecting a little decency into our morally bankrupt society."

"A ten-year-old Maoist!" Horace shouted.

"I'm fifteen," my brother said.

"Listen, boy, capitalists may be dogs, but we're the only dogs that hunt, and if you think—"

At this, Josephine scurried into the den. "Shush." She reminded him that we were still only kids. "Lovey, remember, the sky has yet to fall on their heads."

"They should keep looking up," Horace said.

Yet she calmed him. They could take it all away—every cent, the houses, the honorary degrees, and the lifetime community service medallion from the Fall River Chamber of Commerce. They could put all his heirlooms on the front lawn and he could stand there and watch while the auctioneer yodeled and the neighbors hauled off the family silver for a song, but he was still married to Josephine Sharkansky and you could see that in his watery eyes when she came to rescue my brother. Josephine, with her long blue-gray hair pulled tightly around her head, poured another round of tea into our delicate cups. My grandmother, who had been hovering in the kitchen throughout the visit, clattering pots and reorganizing drawers, emerged and said under her breath, "Jo, how can you serve children tea in the good china?"

"Our mother's service, Sadie's," Josephine said to my grandmother. "You never knew her." My grandmother looked at Josephine, and for a moment the two of them remembered their mother, who must have been something to have given birth to all five of the Sharkansky girls—Molly, Josephine, Haddy, Ida, and my grandmother, the baby. It must have been too much for her. Sadie died before she turned forty.

Horace and Josephine often apologized to my brother and me for not being rich anymore. Josephine would say things like: "Oh, lambs, if things hadn't gone to the absolute dogs, we'd all be on the Cape right now and you two would be splashing in the bay like a couple of little John Johns." As a consolation, they would take us to Horseneck Beach. I remember one time we were pulling into the parking lot on one of those blazy gusty days, the waves a fluster of rising white gush, and Josephine turned to Horace and said, "Oh, Mr. Onassis. You're always taking me places."

Years later, when I was a freshman in high school and my brother was already away at college, I remember standing in the little kitchen on Wampanoag Street, talking to Josephine about books. She thought it scandalous that I hadn't yet read *The Charterhouse of Parma*. How could a boy your age not know Fabrizio? She wanted to know what sort of education I was receiving at public school. Horace had been skulking around, ignoring us. Talk of anything other than politics or business irritated him; he was lonely for my brother. I watched him stoop to pick something up off the kitchen floor. He tickled

Josephine's ankle with a couple of stubby, unsteady fingers. She reached down and, without taking her eyes off me, swatted. Horace muttered and withdrew like a shooed-away crab.

"Oh, it's you," she said. "I thought it was a crawly."

But they couldn't carry on like that forever, and Horace, who was seven years older, eventually got sick. No one in our family ever says what anyone is sick with, sick is sick. Whatever it was, it soon became too serious for Josephine. Aunt Molly had died by this time. So they moved Horace to the Jewish Home for the Aged out on Warren Avenue. And though he never did get much better, Horace didn't die right away, either. He lingered, for years. Whenever I visited Fall River, my grandmother would conspire to keep me busy seeing other relatives, but I overheard things because she was a terrible whisperer. Once, she hid in the bathroom. The phone cord was stretched across the hall and ran under the door. Still, she practically shouted. "I don't know, Haddy. Tuesday he stopped eating." Then Josephine fell down on the icy sidewalk in front of Molly's. They ran tests. Again, nobody talked, but we knew it was bad and that it went beyond a broken hip. My grandmother couldn't get Josephine a bed in the Jewish Home, even though Horace's money had put a new wing on the place back in his salad days. *Ginsburg* was chiseled above the front door. My grandmother stomped around the house. "Waiting list? Our Josephine on a waiting list?" She sat at the kitchen table with the phone book. "I'm going to make some calls." I watched her finger in the rotary, poised to circle. She rammed the phone down.

"Damnit, if he didn't steal from the father, he stole from the son."

"What about Uncle Ira?" I said.

My grandmother stood up. Even in her sweat suit, she was square-shouldered, bulky, formidable. My grandfather had so many names for her: La Duce, Generalissimo Patton. My grandfather'd been dead at least ten years by then.

"Ira Pinkus?" my grandmother said. "May we never sink so low."

She sat down again and stared at the phone book. Horace needed special medical care and couldn't be moved from the Jewish Home. Josephine clearly couldn't live alone. Pauline had just turned eighty herself. My grandmother was stretched too thin driving around caring for Uncle Charlie and Aunt Haddy, both of whom could hardly walk by this time, not to mention Ida in Providence with her kidney trouble. And everybody, old and young, was too broke and too busy. There was no choice but to put Josephine in the state home across the river in Somerset. "It's close enough," my grandmother said. "Just across the Braga Bridge."

My brother told me this last part as we stood blowing into our hands at Josephine's graveside service in the late 1990s. He said not to repeat it. He got it from my mother, who told him not to tell anybody. She'd heard it from my grandmother who'd told her, before she herself died, not to breathe a word to a soul. Stories move through my family in this efficient way. My brother said that a week before Horace's death, a year and a half before Josephine's, two of my Rhode Island cousins, Jacob and Mimi, arranged for Horace and Josephine to say goodbye. At this point, Horace was blind and mostly slept all day, but

Jacob smuggled him into a car—this was all against strict doctor's orders, so it had to be done undercover—and drove him to a shopping center between the two nursing homes. Mimi drove Aunt Josephine, who by then had lost nearly half her body weight. Horace and Josephine hadn't seen each other in two years. The family had been waiting for one or the other to die quietly, but neither would cooperate. He was ninety-five. She was ninety-two. The two cars pulled up, and there they were, Horace and Josephine, in the parking lot of Al Mac's. Josephine was able to stand up and walk slowly over to Horace, who was slumped in the passenger seat. Jacob opened the door and started to help him, but Horace pushed him away. He knew she was close and tried to pull himself out of the seat, but couldn't; so Josephine leaned into the car, and Horace dropped his head on her shoulder. Then she whispered something to him. Neither Jacob or Mimi heard what she said. Maybe she told him she'd meet him wherever he was going and not to worry, they'd be flush when they got there. "Meet me by the roulette wheel in Monte Carlo, at Beaumont's. I'll be the one in the fox coat and white heels." The two of them remained slumped over each other until my cousins finally broke them apart and drove them away in separate cars.

I was six, maybe seven months old, and I had a babysitter named Eva. She was from somewhere in the West Indies and spoke with, my parents always said, the most charming singsong accent you could imagine. My father called her the governess. That night my parents were at the opera. It was February. This is when we lived on Lincoln and Webster, near Oz Park. The heat went out in our building and it got so cold that Eva wrapped me in a towel and put me in the oven. My parents came home from Rigoletto and found Eva jumping in place in the kitchen. On her head was a large furry Russianish hat of my father's. My mother, essentially unalarmable in any circumstances, didn't scream when she realized what was in the oven, though at first she wasn't entirely sure what she was seeing. My father, too, he just took it in. He may have been equally astonished that the governess was wearing his favorite hat. Me? Nobody asked, but had I been able to talk I would have said I was comfortable as hell and that my removal from this new womb was as unwelcome as my previous abduction from the original. Eva had the right idea. The minute I get settled you people come and yank me out—

CHICAGO, 1969

PAMPKIN'S LAMENT

Two-term Governor Cheeky Al Thorstenson was so popular that year that his Democratic challenger could have been, my father said, Ricardo Montalban in his prime and it wouldn't have made a 5 percent difference. Even so, somebody had to run, somebody always has to run, and so Mike Pampkin put his sacrificial head into the race, and my father, equally for no good reason other than somebody must prepare the lamb for the slaughter, got himself hired as campaign manager. Nobody understood it all better than Pampkin himself. He wore his defeat right there on his body, like one of the unflattering V-neck sweaters that made his breasts mound outward like a couple of sad little hills. When he forced himself to smile for photographers, Pampkin always looked slightly constipated. And he was so endearingly, down-homey honest about his chances that people loved him. Of course, not enough to vote for him. Still, for such an ungraceful man, he had long, elegant hands, Jackie O. hands, my father said, only Pampkin's weren't gloved. Mike Pampkin's hands were unsheathed, out in the open for the world to see. He was the loneliest-seeming man ever to run for statewide office in Illinois.

It was 1980. I was a mostly ignored fourteen-year-old and I had already developed great disdain for politics. It bored me to hatred. But if I could have voted, I must say I would have voted for Cheeky Al also. His commercials were very good and I liked his belt buckles. Everybody liked Cheeky Al's belt buckles.

Probably what is most remembered, if anything, about Mike Pampkin during that campaign was an incident that happened in Waukegan during the Fourth of July parade. Pampkin got run over by a fez-wearing Shriner on a motorized flying carpet. The Shriner swore it was an accident, but this didn't stop the *Waukegan News Sun* from running the headline: PAMPKIN SWEPT UNDER RUG.

My memory of that time is of less public humiliation.

One night, it must have been a few weeks before Election Day, there was a knock on our back door. It was after two in the morning. The knock was mousy but insistent. I first heard it in my restless dreams, as if someone were tapping on my skull with a pencil. Eventually, my father answered the door. I got out of bed and went downstairs. I found them facing each other at the kitchen table. If either Pampkin or my father noticed me, they didn't let on. I crouched on the floor and leaned against the cold stove. My father was going on, as only my father could go on. To him, at this late stage, the election had become, if not an actual race, not a total farce, either. The flying-carpet incident had caused a small sympathy bump in the polls, and the bump had held.

Yet it was more than this. Politics drugged my father. He loved nothing more than to hear his own voice holding forth, and he'd work himself up into a hallucinatory frenzy of absolute

certainty when it came to anything electoral. One of my earli-
est memories is of my parents having it out during the '72 presidential primaries. My father had ordained from on high that
Scoop Jackson was the party's savior, the only one who could
rescue the Democrats from satanic George Wallace. My
mother, treasonably, was for Edmund Muskie, that pantywaist.
There were countless other things, but doesn't everything, one
way or another, come down to politics? In my family, politics
isn't blood sport, it's blood itself. Finally, in 1979, my mother,
brother, and I moved out for good, to an apartment across
town. But every other weekend and Wednesday nights I spent
with my father in the house that used to be our house, in the
room that used to be my room, in the bed that used to be my bed.

My father in the kitchen in October of 1980, rattling off to Pampkin what my father called "issue conflagrations," by which he
meant those issues that divided city voters from downstaters. To
my father, anybody who didn't live in Chicago or the suburbs
was a downstater, even if they lived upstate, across state, or on an
island in the Kankakee River. He told Pampkin that his position
on the Zion nuclear power plant was too wishy-washy, that the
anti-nuke loons were getting ready to fry him in vegetable oil.

"Listen, Mike, it doesn't matter that Cheeky Al's all for plu-
tonium in our cheeseburgers. The only meat those cannibals
eat is their own kind."

Pampkin wasn't listening. He was staring out the kitchen
window, at his own face in the glass. He didn't seem tired or
weary or anything like that. If anything, he was too awake. In
fact, his eyes were so huge they looked torn open. Of course,

he knew everything my father was saying. Pampkin wasn't a neophyte. He'd grown up in the bosom of the machine, in the 24th Ward. Izzy Horowitz and Jake Arvey were his mentors. He'd worked his way up, made a life in politics, nothing flashy, steady. Daley himself was a personal friend. And when the mayor asks you to take a fall to Cheeky Al, you take a fall to Cheeky Al. That Daley was dead and buried now didn't make a difference. A promise to Mayor Daley is a promise to Mayor Daley, and there is only one Mayor Daley. Pampkin didn't need my father's issue conflagrations. He was a man who filled a suit. Didn't a man have to fill something? At the time he ran, I think Pampkin was state comptroller, whatever that means.

So the candidate sat mute as my father began to soar, his pen conducting a symphony in the air.

"So we go strong against nuclear power in the city on local TV here. But when you're down in Rantoul on Thursday, make like you didn't hear the question. Stick your finger in your ear. Kiss a baby, anything—"

"Raymond."

Pampkin seemed almost stunned by his own voice. He was calm, but I noticed his cheeks loosen as if he'd been holding my father's name in his mouth. Then he said, "My wife's leaving me. It's not official. She says she won't make it official until after the election. She's in love, she says."

My father dropped his pen. It rolled off the table and onto the floor, where it came to rest against my bare toes. I didn't pick it up. On the table between the two men were precinct maps, charts, phone lists, mailing labels, buttons, and those olive Pampkin bumper stickers so much more common around our house than on cars.

"Can I get you a cup of coffee, Mike?"

I watched my father. He was gazing at Pampkin with an expression I'd never seen before. Drained of his talk, he looked suddenly kinder. Here is a man across this table, a fellow sojourner. What I am trying to say is that it was a strange time — 1980. A terrible time in many ways, and yet my father became at that moment infused with a little grace. Maybe the possibility of being trounced not only by Cheeky Al but also by the big feet of Ronald Reagan himself had opened my father's eyes to the existence of other people. Here was a man in pain.

They sat and drank coffee, and didn't talk about Mrs. Pampkin. At least not with their mouths. With their eyes they talked about her, with their fingers gripping their mugs they talked about her.

Mrs. Pampkin?

My inclination before that night would have been to say that she was as forgettable as her husband. More so. Though I had seen her many times, I couldn't conjure up her face. I remembered she wore earth tones. I remembered she once smelled like bland soap. She wasn't pudgy; she wasn't lanky. She wasn't stiff, nor was she jiggly. Early on in the campaign, my father had suggested to Pampkin that maybe his wife could wear a flower in her hair at garden events, or at the very least lipstick for television. Nothing came of these suggestions, and as far as I knew, the issue of Pampkin's wife hadn't come up again until that night in the kitchen, when, for me, she went from drab to blazing. She'd done something unexpected. If Mrs. Pampkin was capable of it, what did this mean for the rest of us? I remembered — then — that I had watched her after Mike got hit by the carpet. She hadn't become hysterical. She'd merely walked over to him lying there on the pavement (the Shriner apologizing over and over), and the expression in her eyes was of such motionless calm that Mike and everybody else around knew it was going to be all right, that this was only another humiliation in the long line that life hands us, nothing more, nothing less. She'd knelt to him.

Pampkin's hand crept across the table toward my father's. Gently he clutched my father's wrist.

"Do you know what she said? She said, 'You have no idea how this feels.' I said, 'Maureen, I thought I did.'"

"More coffee, Mike?"

"Please."

But he didn't let go of my father's wrist, and my father didn't try to pull it away. Pampkin kept talking.

"You get to a point you think you can't be surprised. I remember a lady once, a blind lady. Lived on Archer. Every day she went to the same store up the block. Every day for thirty-five years. She knows this stretch of block as if she laid the cement for the sidewalk herself. It's her universe. One day they're doing some sewage work and some clown forgets to replace the manhole cover and vamoose. She drops. Crazy that she lived. Broke both legs. It cost the city four hundred thousand on the tort claim to settle it. I'm talking about this kind of out-of-nowhere."

My father sat there and watched him.

"Or let's say you're on Delta. Sipping a Bloody Mary. Seatbelt sign's off. There's a jolt. Unanticipated turbulence, they call it. It happened to a cousin of Vito Marzullo. All he was trying to do was go to Philadelphia. Broke his neck on the overhead bin."

*　　*　　*

When I woke up on the kitchen floor, the room looked different, darker, smaller in the feeble light of the sun just peeping over the bottom edge of the kitchen window. Pampkin was still sitting there, gripping his mug of cold coffee and talking across the table to my father's shaggy head, which was facedown and drooling on the bumper stickers. My father was young then. He's always looked young; even to this day, his gray sideburns seem more like an affectation than a sign of age. But early that morning he really was young, and Pampkin was still telling my father's head what it was like to be surprised. And he didn't look any more rumpled than usual. Now, when I remember all this, I think of Fidel Castro, who still gives those eighteen-hour speeches to the party faithful. There on the table, my father's loyal head.

I was fourteen and I woke up on the floor with a hard-on over Mrs. Pampkin. One long night on the linoleum had proved that lust, if not love, had a smell, and that smell was of bland soap. I thought of ditching school and following her to some apartment or a Red Roof Inn. I wanted to watch them. I wanted to see something that wasn't lonely. Tossed-around sheets, a belt lying on the floor. I wanted to know what they said, how they left each other, who watched the retreating back of the other. How do you part? Why would you ever? Even for an hour? Even when you know that the next day, at some appointed hour, you will have it again?

Got to go. My husband's running for governor.

Pampkin droned on. He had his shoes off and was sitting there in his mismatched socks, his toes quietly wrestling each other.

"Or put it this way. An old tree. Its roots are dried up. But you can't know this. You're not a botanist, a tree surgeon, or Smokey the Bear. One day, a whiff of breeze comes and topples it. Why that whiff?"

I couldn't hold back a loud yawn, and Pampkin looked down at me on the floor. He wasn't startled by the rise in my shorts. He wasn't startled by anything anymore.

He asked me directly, "You. Little fella. You're as old as Methuselah and still you don't know squat about squat?"

I shrugged.

Pampkin took a gulp of old coffee. "Exactly," he said. "Exactly."

And either I stopped listening or he stopped talking, because after a while his voice got faint and the morning rose for good.

Pampkin died twelve years later, in the winter of '92. (The obituary headline in the *Chicago Sun-Times* ran: AMIABLE POLITICIAN LOST GOVERNOR'S RACE BY RECORD MARGIN.) I went with my father to the funeral. The Pampkins had never divorced. We met Mrs. Pampkin on the steps of the funeral home in Skokie. All it took was the way they looked at each other. I won't try to describe it, except to say that it lasted too long and had nothing to do with anybody—or anything—newly dead. They didn't touch. They didn't need to. They watched each other's smoky breath in the chill air. Facing her in her grief and her wide-brimmed black hat, my father looked haggard and puny. He turned away only after more people came up to her to offer condolences. I don't know how long it went on between them. I'm not even sure it matters. Does it? I now know it's easier to walk away from what you thought you couldn't live without than I had once imagined.

She was taller than I remembered. Her face was red with sadness and January.

"Don't look so pale, Ray," she whispered to my father before moving on to the other mourners, her hand hovering for a moment near his left ear. "Mike always thought you were a good egg."

LINCOLN

That year we lived on W Street in a small one-story house with a concrete slab in the backyard. Everybody else on our block lived in similar houses, and during the long summer we spent afternoons sitting in chairs on our respective slabs. In the Midwest, we don't appreciate fences. Yards should blend into yards. I don't remember any of our neighbors' names, only that we sometimes drank a few beers together and talked about the heat. There are so many ways to talk about heat. I was an adjunct in the English Department. Sam was a poet who didn't believe universities and poetry had anything to do with each other. She got a job at the Golden Wok, waiting tables. The Golden Wok was cheap and open late, a big sprawling place that had a way of looking empty even when it was filled with people. It was there she met someone, whether a fellow waiter or a patron, I never asked. Lincoln used to be a beautiful city. This was before it got ruined, locals said, by too many expressways. Nebraska, apparently, can never have enough roads through it. Still, there were the sunken gardens with all the flowers in a bowl and the mansions up on Sheridan Boulevard. Sam and I would drive up there and look at the houses. Once, she pointed to one of the houses and said, in all seriousness, Who would we be if we lived there?

"Couple of rich-ass Nebraskans," I said.

"That's all?"

Sometimes I think of that house. It had what Sam called a porte cochere over the driveway. Sam was from the South and said such dumb open garages were common in South Carolina.

"They're for hairdos, you know, to protect the ladies when it's raining."

Near our house on W Street there was a park with a couple of netless tennis courts, and I used to sit at a picnic table under the tall trees and read for class. I remember sitting there and reading the Time Passes sections of *To the Lighthouse* and coming, again, to that moment when Mr. Ramsey reaches out for Mrs. Ramsey in the dark of the morning corridor, not knowing that she's already gone. That she died alone during the night. It happened, like so many things, off stage. But Mrs. Ramsey? How could it still jolt? That loss? The tall trees, nobody playing tennis.

LAST CAR OVER
THE SAGAMORE BRIDGE

In the unquiet of his shoe-box study, amid the noises of his house, Walt tries to read. Walt Kaplan. Furniture salesman, daydreamer, reader. It's 1947, a year no one will much remember. After the war, but before anybody really got used to the war being over. He gives up. How could anybody read in this asylum? The peck of the clock nicks away his flesh. No matter how much I eat, he thinks, it makes no difference. I'm a fat husk. A funny thing. Sarah's downstairs on the phone: the phone. Such fathomless yappery. Why, *why* must she shout? Is everyone who rings this house in need of orders? And there is the thump of Miriam's battering up and down the stairs. Eight years old and the kid sounds like a platoon. And he aches for her. He always has. So that somehow hearing her is the same as not hearing her is the same as her gone. What? Kid this loud? Possible? Gone? Such cacophony. I am a morbid man, a morbid, lazy sloucher. He shouts, "Knock it off, Orangutan! You got a father in here thinking." The kid doesn't answer. So he talks to Sarah without talking to Sarah, which is one of the great advantages of being married so long. Cuts down on the need for superflous conversation. He talks to the idea of her. She talks on the phone.

I'm talking fundamentals, Sarah, follow me? You make something in this world, take, yes, a child, and then? Then?

Don't be daft. We got bills to pay and cocktails at the Dolinskys' at eight.

Dolinskys? What could we possibly have to say to them that hasn't been said?

We can't be late. Doris made reservations at the Lobster Pot for quarter to nine.

So much for mine wife's wise counsel. Not that I don't enjoy a good cocktail as much as the next man. Glenlivet for me, thanks. Nobody can say Walt Kaplan's not a classy egg. But listen: What I'm getting at is silence and what it means in a world where there's not any, at least we think there's not any, but we got a whole lot coming, you know? I tell the kid, Knock it off, Orangutan, you got a father in here thinking…and if the kid heard, which even if she did, she didn't, she might have stopped at my door and spoken through the keyhole and said, Thinking about what, Daddy? And I might have said, I'm remembering things, which is hard work. You think remembering things is a peanut, Peanut?

Remembering what?

Lot of things. For instance the hurricane of '38, when I, your father—

That story!

You think a story dies?

(Her little mouth breathing through the keyhole.) Five hundred times I've heard that same story.

Five hundred and one, five hundred and two, five hundred and three. Your mother is home here in Fall River, and you and

I, Orangutan, are out on the Cape at Horace's place in Dennis. A little father and daughter vacation from the dragon, and the dragon calling up and squawking, *Didn't you hear the weather? Get out of there! Evacuate! You'll get swept to—*

China, the kid would say through the keyhole. We're always getting swept to China in this family.

Precisely! And Walt Kaplan knows who's boss. The man takes good orders, and he blankets you up. You were two years old and your feet were like a short fat man's thumbs. I ever tell you that? That your feet were like a short fat man's thumbs? Every time you tell anything, you have to add something new. And your father, great and fearless father, carries his daughter to the mainland in his Chrysler Imperial steed. Last car over the Sagamore Bridge before the hurricane of '38 sent half the Cape into the Atlantic. They called it the Long Island Express. New Yorkers got to have their nose in everything. They even take our disasters. Rhode Island, blew away, too, but nobody noticed. What's half of Rhode Island anway? Is your mother never wrong? No—she hasn't got the time. She's got Louise Greenbaum on the line. *Paging Sarah Kaplan. Sarah Kaplan. Louise Greenbaum on the line.* So, yes, hail the Sultana! But salute the infantryman, too. Walt Kaplan, hero of the Sagamore Bridge. Write him down as a footnote in the annals, hearty scribes!

And so Walt sits in the unstillness of his shoe-box study and thinks about fundamentals.

You make a kid, and the wind comes and tries to air mail it to Asia. Insurance got Horace a new house. The claim: Act of God. Act of God? State Farm's going to send me a new kid? That only happens in the Book of Job. Last car, Walt Kaplan, dodges the terrible wrath of wraths, but how many more to come? How many acts has God got left? What on earth compares with the shame of not being able to protect your daughter, your only only? Let a father weep in peace, Orangutan. That fuckin' thumping. Hellion child. The devil's spawn. Sarah, my yappery-yapperer. Not the clock that dooms us, but the us of us. We're walking, talking Acts of God. Don't you get it? The thumping will not echo. It only booms in the brain, in the silence which is nowhere. A grave has more hold than the noise of this house. Miriam's feet tromp up and down the stairs. You say I don't get out enough, that I waste my life's blood cooped up here being morbid, being stupid. Sarah? Sarah? You hearing me?

The kid's gonna die, Walt. I'm gonna die. You're gonna die. Tell me something else, you genuis.

Don't laugh at me, woman.

Youwantmetostartweepingnow?Thisminute?Wegotcocktails—

That's it. I'm asking you, I'm really asking you—how is it possible that we aren't in a permanent state of mourning?

I ironed you a shirt. It's on the bathroom knob.

Would my head were a head of lettuce. I drove the last car over the Sagamore Bridge before the state police closed it off. The Cape Cod Canal all atempest beneath. No cars coming, no cars going. The bridge cables flapping like rubber bands. You think in certain circumstances a few thousand feet of bridge isn't a thousand miles? The hurricane wiped out Dennis. Horace thanked God for insurance. I saved our little girl. You want me to say, Hurrah! Hurrah! but I can't, I won't, because to save her once isn't to save her, and still she thumps as if the world was something thumpable. As if it wasn't silence on a fundamental level. Yap on, wife, yap on. Thump, daughter, thump. Louder, Orangutan, louder. I can't hear you.

PART II

The Normal

NATHAN LEOPOLD WRITES TO
MR. FELIX KLECZKA OF
5383 S. BLACKSTONE

Castaner, Puerto Rico (Associated Press, April 7, 1958)

Nathan Leopold is learning the technique of his 10 dollar a month laboratory job in the hospital here and using most of his spare time to answer his voluminous mail. One hospital official said the paroled Chicago slayer has received 2,800 letters in the three weeks he has been here, from all parts of the United States. He has expressed his intentions to answer every letter.

The room is not as bare as you might imagine. In fact, it's crowded. A distant relative in the furniture business shipped a load of overstock from the Merchandise Mart. Sofas, love seats, end tables, floor lamps, a pool table. It took three trucks to deliver it all from San Juan.

Nathan, home from work, sits at a large oak desk, big as a banker's. He takes off his shoes. He rubs his feet awhile. He watches his canaries. The birds are, for a change, silent. He leaves their cage door open. He likes to watch them sleep, their heads up, their eyes vaguely open, as if on a whim they could fly in their dreams.

He takes another letter from the pile and sets it in front of him. He puts on his glasses. He reads.

When he's finished, he brings his hand to his face and gently rests his index finger on the tip of his nose. The room has a single window that looks out upon the village and, beyond it, a small mountain. When he first arrived here, it was heaven. The spell was short-lived. He no longer feels the urge to walk across the village to the mountain and climb it.

Dear Mr. Kleczka,

I received your correspondence two weeks ago. Please accept my most sincere apologies. I receive a great many letters and am doing my best to reply with a reasonable degree of promptness. Also, note that the mail delivery services here in the hills outside San Juan leave a bit to be desired. Among other things, you call me God's revulsion and express the wish that I choke on my poisonous froth. You write that my employment in a hospital is the ghastliest joke Satan ever played and, as a veteran of Hitler's war, you know from whence you speak. I do not doubt you. You write from what you describe as the old neighborhood. Let's not indulge ourselves. I am not going to tell you about the last thirty-three years. I want you to know that I believe—I am sure this is something even we can agree on—I am the luckiest man in the world. I am free and nothing you could imagine is more delirious. Yet, delirium, I might add, always gives way to a fog that never lifts. This said, allow me to describe a bit of my work at the hospital. I met a woman today. She is dying of a rare disease. It is not pancreatic cancer, the doctor assured me, but something far more uncommon. The disease is untreatable, and the most that can be done for this woman is to prescribe painkillers and ensure a constant supply of nutrients to the bloodstream, because, apparently—this is the way I understand it—her body rejects those fluids necessary for the survival of her vital organs. In other words the patient is leaking away. Her name is Maya de Hostas and she has two children, Javier and Theresa. There is no husband to speak of. Maya de Hostas is dying, Mr. Kleczka, but it is a slow process. The doctor says it could take more than six months, perhaps a year. Do you scoff? Do you tear at this paper? Do your hands flutter with rage? Nathan Leopold is telling a story. Nathan Leopold is telling a story of other people suffering. You remember my youthful arrogance like it was yesterday. All the brains they said I had. All the books I'd read, all the languages they said I spoke. Russian, Greek, Arabic. They say I even knew Sanskrit! My famous attorney glibly talking away the rope. I still repeat his speech like a prayer. The easy and the popular thing to do is to hang my clients. *It is men like you, men with long memories, that make our—your—city great. You sweep the streets of scum like me. This is no defense, Mr. Kleczka of 5383 S. Blackstone, but allow me to tell you I love you. I love you for keeping the torch lit, for taking the time to write to me. I am deadly serious, oh* deadly serious, and as I sit here—the waning moments of light purpling the mountains—I imagine you. I imagine you reading of my parole with such beautiful fury. You want to come here yourself and mete out justice. Don't you want to get on a plane and come and murder me with your own bare hands? No gloves for such a fiend. And then take a vacation. Why not? Bring the wife and kids. It's Puerto Rico. But your wife says an eye for eye wouldn't help anybody and certainly wouldn't make any difference to Bobby Franks. It wouldn't bring that angel back, and they'd only throw the key away on you. (Though, of course, your defense would have much to say by way of mitigation.) But the monster, you cried. Animal! Your wife is a wise woman but you, Sir, are wiser. There are times, of course, when only blood will suffice. Should you make the trip, know that my door is always open. I live in a two-room flat. If I'm absent at my employment, please wait for me. Make yourself at home. Don't mind the chatter of the canaries. I feed them in the morning. I keep whiskey, though the conditions of my parole forbid spirits, in my third desk drawer. Why not pour yourself a glass? And know that as you strangle me or slash my throat or simply blow my head off, I'll love you. As I bleed onto this unswept floor (the maid comes only on Tuesdays), I'll love you. Mr. Felix Kleczka of the old neighborhood. What else can I say to you? Do not for a moment think I say any of this slyly. I have been waiting with open eyes and open arms for the last thirty-three years, prepared to die the same death as Dickie Loeb, whose rank flesh is only less tainted than mine for being done away with sooner. Only maggots know the *truth. Well, I am here. I will never hide from you. I get a great deal of mail, as I said. Much of it is supportive of my new life. This week alone I received three marriage proposals. Your letter reminded me very starkly of who and what I am. Even so, I must ask you: Are there still old neighborhoods? Are there still people who knew us when? And should you decide not to come and take up the knife against me, know that I think no less of you. Your cowardice, more than anything, this I understand. Once, a young man bludgeoned a child with a chisel. To make certain, I stuffed my fist in his mouth. My hands are rather plump now. Still, even now, I recognize them for what they are, some days.*

Sincerely,

N. Leopold

The dark outside the window now. He's lived so long craving it. It was the light, all that light. He thinks now that he —

Now that he what?

He flicks on the lamp for comfort. He watches his face in the window. His laugh begins softly, like a murmur. Eventually it will be loud enough to wake the birds.

*A*t the end of our street was a commune in a log mansion—Jed Holson's house—and girls in frayed orange cable-knit sweaters and no pants would chase each other across its huge furnitureless rooms. It was the suburbs, it was the seventies, life was bizarre and glorious, and we didn't even know it. Jed's father, Elijah Holson, had been a founding director of the Chicago, Rock Island and Pacific Railroad. In 1918, he built himself an eighteen-room house of locally hand-hewn oak on a bluff overlooking Lake Michigan. He dug a moat around the house and put down a drawbridge. A grand house, a famous house, a house for the ages. The son was even more eccentric. In the spirit of his own time, past seventy himself, Jed Holson went hippie. His wife fled to California, and Jed opened his father's mythical log palace to all female comers. Longhaired men were welcome, too. The lawn was crowded with VW buses and tents. People did their laundry in the moat. Jed's doctor lawyer banker neighbors didn't know what to make of all the parties. It didn't matter. They weren't invited. By the time I was old enough to enjoy the show, Jed—his crazy beard, his experiment in alternative living, his passel of nymphs—was forgotten. The log house went dark. Free love, old hat. Did pantsless girls ever chase each other? I could swear. Plus, my *brother told me. And as a kid, I used to climb up and pace the front porch, ghosting back and forth in front of the big windows, waiting for the flesh and the laughter. Jed must have been asleep somewhere in the gloom, his chin a tangle of yellow beard.*

HIGHLAND SARK, ILLINOIS, 1981

DETAMBLE

They tore down the house on Detamble, but this has never mattered. We see that house every time we drive by. It happened more than thirty years ago. A childless couple. A childless couple who had always, the *Sun-Times* quoted a neighbor as saying, kept to themselves. Did they truly keep to themselves? Or is it only with hindsight that we see such people in their isolation? The husband was a retired ear, nose, and throat specialist; the wife was a horticulturist at the Chicago Botanic Gardens on Lake Cook Road. It might have taken them longer to find them if not for the dog. On the night of the third day, the hunger got to be too much, and her howling finally alarmed the neighbors. They went over and rang the bell. When they got no answer, they called the police, who used an ax to break in a side door. The husband and wife were found in the garage. (The dog, an Afghan hound, was found locked in the basement.) The only signs of struggle were bloody scratches on the wife's arms and cheeks. The husband had no defensive wounds. This led investigators to conjecture that he had been taken by surprise, while she had seen it all coming. The other clues were that both of them had their heads stove in by either some type of batlike object or the fireplace poker, the only material thing, as far as anybody could tell, missing from the house. A last piece of compelling piece of evidence: the wife, the horticulturalist, was found wearing a money belt that still contained $20,000 cash.

"Bookies," our neighbor to the east and town opinionator Penny Shumager surmised. "Everybody knows, after a certain point, it's too late to pay them back with money. And I, for one, always knew something wasn't right about those two. Why no kids? People who live in the suburbs without kids to raise are always hiding something. Why else would they live here?"

Penny Schumager may have had something there, and this is pretty much how we all took it. Must have been some kind of gambling debt. Don't mess with the mob. You think they respect a suburban border? You think they care this is Lake County? No matter how mild-mannered you seem, they'll take care of business the only way they know how.

There are no more memorable details and no other reasons to remember this couple aside from the way they died. We hadn't known them. We hadn't even known them well enough to make up stories about them, except of course Penny Shumager, who never had any compunction about making up stories about anybody, murdered or unmurdered.

It is tempting, after so long, the file long since closed, to zero in on the dog. Dogs are sympathetic. In a lot of stories dogs are even more sympathetic than people. For hours and hours, there's that confused, whimpering, sleeping, pacing, foraging, and finally hopelessly yowling dog. Maybe the story is the dog and how alone she was, and how silent the house seemed. Those two had always been quiet, but no voices at all is different from silence. The silence worried the dog more than hunger. The woman had a small sad way of laughing that the dog could always hear wherever she happened to be in the house. The dog would always run toward that laugh.

It should be said that the murders, in spite of their brutality, didn't terrorize us. We didn't lock our doors any more than we had before. Everybody knew this wasn't the beginning of a crime wave. No omen. It was simply an aberration. Our town has always been a safe place to raise your kids. Detamble, like so many of our leafy streets, is peaceful. Nothing ever happens on Detamble. It's mathematical. But don't you need some sort of break in the normal for there to be normal in the first place? The normal, the leafy, the peaceful reaches out and bludgeons. A kind of sacrifice so the rest of us can slumber on amid the trees, on the bluffs, by the lake.

DYKE BRIDGE

Chappaquiddick, Massachusetts, 1976

My brother and I in the knee-deep water, standing in the tidal current, under Dyke Bridge. We are hunting whelks. It is the water Mary Jo Kopechne drowned in. I know all about it. About Teddy drunk and how the story of what happened was less covered up than simply muddled. What was there to cover up? Her body was found in his car. My brother told me. How Teddy was still mourning his brothers, both his brothers, and that he drank too much. Not that this excuses what happened, my brother says. But wouldn't you drink if somebody shot me in the head? And then your other brother? If you had another brother? In the head also? Wouldn't you drink a whole hell of a lot and probably crash a car?

We are on vacation with our parents on Martha's Vineyard. We are from Illinois. It is classy, according to my parents, if you are from Illinois to take a vacation on Martha's Vineyard. It's also Kennedyesque. My parents are still married (to each other), though my brother and I would prefer this not to be the case. We have ridden our bikes out to this bridge to see this very spot, to muck around in this famous water. My brother is wearing a T-shirt with the face of Sam Ervin, hero of the Watergate hearings.

I want to remember that we were alone, that it was only the two of us, but somewhere, in some stack of pictures, in some cabinet in my father's house, there are pictures of my brother and me standing under Dyke Bridge, so it must be that at least one of our parents was with us and recorded it, and since my mother rarely took pictures, it had to have been my father; but let's leave him out of this. Just my brother and me in the knee-deep water and my brother telling me that Teddy was heading back to the island that night, back from the even smaller island where they'd been at a party. That he was driving a black Chevrolet, because the Kennedys may be richer than Howard Hughes but they aren't ostentatious. That's class. And that Mary Jo Kopechne wasn't even very beautiful. She wasn't Teddy Kennedy's wife, either, he says, but that goes with this territory.

What territory?

The territory of being richer than God, my brother says. The landscape of sex and whisperings and innuendo.

I would rather fish up a whelk than listen to this, a live whelk with the black body inside, a Jell-O-ish squirmy thing that we will take back to our rented house and boil alive on the stove.

Even so, I ask, how much not very beautiful was she?

And my brother says, Not particularly unbeautiful. Just not that beautiful for a Kennedy. She wasn't Jackie, is what I'm trying to say. But anyway, nobody was Jackie. Even Jackie wasn't Jackie. Anyway, Teddy may have even loved her though he hardly knew her.

But still, Teddy may have even loved her, even though he hardly knew her. Especially after she drowned.

What do you mean?

My brother stares at me for a while. He and I have the same eyes, which is sometimes creepy. You don't know yourself coming and going, as my grandmother used to say. Then he squats in the water and takes up a couple of handfuls of ocean water and raises his hands as it flows through his fingers. I often remember this, my brother lifting the ocean like that.

Our bikes are on the bridge, leaning against a broken piling. Dyke Bridge is tiny, a miniature bridge. It is not much bigger than the width of a Chevy and nearly the same length. Driving off it is the bathroom equivalent of falling out of the bathtub.

I e-mail my brother and ask him if he remembers all this. He is still very sensitive when it comes to the Kennedys. Like my mother, he remains a staunch believer in the notion that the New England wisdom embodied by the Kennedys and their aristocracy of sorrow will save this doomed country yet.

Why exaggerate? Why tell it worse? What happened isn't enough? Yes, it's a dinky bridge, but it's bigger than a bathtub. I remember. We were out there with Dad. He took pictures. He thought the whole thing was hilarious. He kept saying, Be careful not to step on Mary Jo's face. You were annoyed because he kept saying you had to hold still for the picture. Why don't you ever pick up the phone and call me?

I write: E-mail gives the illusion of dramatic distance. Pretend I'm in Shanghai or somewhere.

He replies: Anyway, isn't anything drive-offable if you put your mind to it? Or even when you don't, especially when you don't? He

was tanked, what's the story? You're gonna pass judgement?
Look at your own life.

My brother is right. He is right. Even when he is not right,
he is right. Look at my own life. And nothing he has ever told
me have I forgotten.

It is only that something happened there, under that bridge,
where my brother and I once swam. As things do, as they always
have, so many more things (strange things, impossible things)
than we can even begin to imagine. Dream it up; it's already happened. One minute you're drunk and laughing and your hand is
on her bare summer thigh and there's nothing but tonight ahead,
and the next, the hood of the car is in the sand and water's flow-
ing in through the cracks in the windows and the car's like a big
fat grounded fish and there's this woman—what's her name
again?—flailing her arms in the dark water and trying to shout
but no sound is coming out of her mouth, and you wonder for a
moment if you love her. *Wait, what's your name?* I'm confused.
This is all so much black confusion. Wait, I can't breathe.
Shouldn't I be swimmingly noble? Don't I know the cross-chest
carry? Aren't I a Kennedy? Aren't I the brother of the hero of
PT-109? Isn't now the time? No. Now is not the time. Now is the
time to save yourself. Doesn't matter who you are, Senator, save
yourself—and run. This I've learned on my own. Sometimes
you just have to save yourself and then run like hell. There'll
always be time for nobility, honor, sorrow, remorse, yes, maybe
even love—in the morning.

The shadow of that little bridge over our heads. Us in the
dark water, my brother and me, the gummy sand, July 1976.

THE MAYOR'S DREAM

No man is an Ireland.

— RICHARD J. DALEY,
48TH MAYOR OF CHICAGO

His Honor's dreams tended to be practical and concerned matters such as tax policy or the loosening of onerous zoning restrictions or who to slate for state's attorney. This was different. He found himself pounding on the door of a house, an ordinary bungalow. For some reason, he wasn't able to use his fists. He'd lost the ability to close his hands. And so with open palms he pounded. Of course, it was his own house at Thirty-sixth and Lowe. Except at first he didn't seem to know this. He tried to pound harder, his hands hopelessly platting against the door. Sis isn't home, nor are the children. He has no keys, apparently no pockets, either. He goes around the house. Same thing. Back door's locked. He's starting to worry that the neighbors will think he is a prowler. He has influence? He knows President Johnson? He knows the Queen of England? *Bring the kids next time, Lizzie.* Right now he is only a man, Dick Daley, and he's locked out of his house. Try throwing your weight around in a dream and see where it gets you. He goes around to the front again and sits on the stoop. Night comes without any slowness. It's day. It's dark. He sits on the stoop. The lights pop on in the house across the street, and he watches the shadows beyond the curtains. He watches those shadows — the Cowleys' shadows — for what feels like hours. Now he wants to know something. Why do shadows dance when if you look directly at the people themselves — not their shadows — they aren't dancing?

FOURTEEN-YEAR-OLDS, INDIANA DUNES, LATE AFTERNOON

Her name is Allie and she sits outside a ring of boys at the bottom of this hill of sand, along the southern edge of Lake Michigan. Chicago rises like a kingdom in the distance. Closer, maybe a quarter of a mile away, lurk the boxy towers of a defunct steel mill. Out in the water is a platform with a rusty crane, floating with no apparent purpose. She wonders how long it has been since the crane has been useful and whether it will ever be useful again. Allie hugs her shoulders and inhales the clean, mineral waft. The lake, for some reason, has always smelled like rice to her.

She used to love one of the boys—Marcus—but it's become clear to her that it isn't Marcus but all the boys together that she loves, wants. Their motley collection of skinny bodies. Alone, she could take or leave any one of them, but together there is something so skittery about them. They all want her, too, or at least they claim to, with their sagging mouths. But would they even know what to do with her body if she tried to give it to them? She's long known what to do with theirs, and she lets them know, and this makes them nervous and need to grip each other harder. It is each other they need. Later, maybe, her. Later one or the other of them will fumble for her in the dark. Now it is only this unfinished day, the sun like a fiery headlight through the trees on the top of the bluff, and the sand, the waves riding slowly up the beach. Wave after wave breaks and flattens, but the noise of them never pauses for even a single breath. That low, constant roar that she will hear long after they all leave this beach. It is each other they need, and it is their needing each other that she wants. She sits on the sand and watches. They wrestle and chase; they smash their bodies into each other. She cups some sand and drains it on her feet. She scratches her long legs. She digs a groove in the sand with her heel and waits to be noticed. Marcus locks arms with Anthony, lifts him up, Anthony's big feet waving. It will go away, this time. Just like the nicknames her father used to call her. Now that she has breasts, he calls her Allison. She stands up and runs down to the edge of the water. She dives, leaving her eyes open. The cold stings. She swims through the blur. The boys have a new thing they say: Butter my bread. Butter it, butter it. She'd do it, faster than they could even imagine. They'd run up the dunes like in a horror movie, screaming for their mothers. Butter nothing, wimps. For now, let them lie about it. For now, let them stay skinny cowards flinging into each other. She rises and stands in the shallow water and faces the beach as the waves break upon the shore, only to fall back toward her.

THE DIVORCE

Gary died before the divorce was finalized, before he'd even moved out. Francine tried to be philosophical about it. Gary, had he been here to laugh, would have laughed. To him matters of life and death were laughable. He'd only fall apart when he couldn't find his keys. And she did try to be — what? — light about the whole thing. An odd word, light, especially as it applied to her. Francine wasn't light; she had no lightness about her. If you asked people, they might have said, Oh, no, not light, whatever you mean by this. Franny's, you know, serious, lovely but serious. And yet today she feels oddly buoyant. Even the casket itself seems as if it's bobbing in water. She loved him. Some people you come across in this world you end up loving. So many we don't. So many we don't even give a second thought. Why Gary? Nothing in particular doomed their marriage, and maybe this is why they decided to end it formally in the eyes of the State of Michigan before they had a true reason they could quantify in their heart of hearts. Heart of hearts. Her mother used to say that. What did it mean, the heart of a heart? What about the heart of a heart of a heart? Where does it stop? She stands before the casket and tries to weep. She's finding it hard to stay focused. Affairs on both sides, but these were years ago, and, if anything, they'd strengthened their bond. For a while they were more interesting to each other. Once she'd run into him on the street downtown and he wasn't wearing his wedding ring and she'd punched him in the face. Gary laughed, she laughed. To the end, he'd made her laugh. Francine wasn't light, but Gary could make her laugh. This is more baffling than sad. I said I wanted to be alone, not alone alone. Gary? Just this past weekend he was packing boxes and asking politely if he should take or leave the ashtray they'd stolen from the hotel in Florence. Neither smoked anymore. What happened to smoking? She keeps trying to weep. She's in the seat of honor, the seat closest to the body of the deceased. Deceased? What kind of word? Isn't it redundant? Why not simply ceased? The casket is just far enough away so that she can't reach out and touch it. She wishes she came from the sort of people who fling themselves on caskets. She saw that once, at the funeral of a Filipino coworker. Relatives clinging all over the casket like people on a raft. The lack of restraint was inspiring. But her own position now is somewhat awkward. Most of their friends know what's been going on. Their kids too, of course. They'd taken it in stride. All in their twenties and thirties now, they'd been trained well by their parents never to pass judgment. Mom, Dad, do what you have to do. We totally get it. Anyway, who's not divorced? People were groping for her now, tugging at her clothes, as if she were a talisman. "Oh, Franny, I'm so, so, so—" "Gary and I were supposed to play golf on Tuesday, a thing like this you can't—" "The soul of kindness, you remember when he came over in his pajamas and talked Arthur off the roof?" "Anything at all, Fran, day or night, call me, will you? You won't. Will you?"

And when it's over she goes home, takes off her dress, and stands before the mirror in what should have been their bedroom. What is this room now? He'd been sleeping in one of the kid's old rooms while he apartment hunted, a phrase he took literally. Gary was hunting down a house, a place to land. He said it was actually interesting, hilarious almost, how even familiar rooms, even architecture you know in the bones of your fingers, can one day simply deny you. Now I'm a guest, now I take up space. Oh, Gary, I just want to be alone, a little alone. Is this such a crime? I'm not blaming you, I'm merely remarking on the situation as a general matter, Fran. It's not about you and me even, it's simply bizarre to be looking for an apartment in a city I thought I knew but don't really, that's what's so...She will have to get dressed again to go to his sister's. Judy had been generous to host the after-funeral, given that it might be uncomfortable for the mourners to see his stuff already packed up like this. She puts on a dress. Hates it, tears it off. She remains in front of the mirror. Now she weeps, out-loud sobs that embarrass her even though it's only her and the cat. Baldo. Baldo purring on the bed like nothing's different. And Gary the only one who truly loves — loved — you. He was trying to find an apartment that accepted pets, which he said wasn't so easy. When did everybody turn on pets? Renters don't get companions? Only owners? How much damage can one old cat possibly do? A lot, she'd said. Don't you remember what Baldo did to the suede couch? It was like Charlie Manson came over. She looks at herself in the mirror. Not so terrible. Her arms need work, but not so bad. She will be wanted again. I will be wanted. She begins to quake before the mirror. Will be wanted. Naked, Gary was always nervous. He'd always been self-conscious of what he considered his small penis. How did he know it was small? Did he go around comparing at the gym? He never went to the gym. She has to remember to cancel his membership. Charlene Gooch moved to New Hampshire to be closer to her grandkids, and they charged her credit card for three years before she noticed. Sex? Not unloving, hasty, and they liked it that way. They'd turn on the light again, begin reading where they'd left off, their bare arms touching. Okay for you? Mmmmmm. You? Mmmmm. My god, she thinks, I'm horny? Now? This is ridiculous. All you were doing was moving out of the house, Gary, not off the face of—

He'd loaded his boxes, not in anger, in bemusement, holding items up, asking, Do you mind? This pillow with the elephant on it is definitely yours. And the furry slippers. *The furry slippers are yours, Gary.* He was magnanimous about the wedding gift crockery. He left her all the good saucepans. He packed only what he was going to need for a small one-bedroom. Still, she could sneak a few things back now, she supposed; by law it was all hers, again. The painting, for instance. He'd packed it with Styrofoam peanuts. They'd had a friend once, an angry aspiring painter. The friend had painted what he called an abstract portrait of the two of them. To Fran and Gary it looked a mound, a blue mound. Still, they'd held on to it, hung it in a corner of the bedroom in case their friend became famous. He was certainly angry enough to be famous. You take it. No, you, he was your friend to begin with. What happened to Yari? People, they evaporate. She stands before the mirror.

But somebody who was just here? How do you remember someone who was here a minute ago? All she wanted, after so many years, was just to be alone. Gary used to sit at the kitchen table and read her things out of the paper. The other day he said something about Egypt. Something about the Suez. How it all started with the Suez Canal. Canals, he said, usually cause more problems than they solve. Why do you think that is? She hadn't answered, only took another sip of coffee and went out to the garage.

1979

Jimmy Carter dead in the water, and the Democrats either can wait to be kicked like a sleeping dog or at least try to bite back. It's 1979 and certain pipe dreams are still smoked. And Ted Kennedy shouts — call it the last gasp of the sixties — *Mutiny!* And Chicago mayor Jane Byrne, Mayor Bossy, Fighting Jane, backs him to the hilt. Byrne relishes any fight. In private, she calls Carter a *psalm-singing son-of-a-bitch.* In public, she says she wants his presidential head on a platter for the good of Chicago, and as Chicago goes, so goes the country. So Byrne hosts a huge fundraiser for Kennedy in the ballroom at the Hyatt Regency. Giddy, rebellious Chicagoans gather to meet the Last Brother. Some people attend because they actually support him; other people want to see who is supporting him in order to decide if they support him. Since nobody can quite figure out who is who, it's a confusing evening. My parents are there. As is Kennedy himself, even though in an interview on CBS, he couldn't for the life of him explain why he was running. *Senator, could you tell the American people why you want to be President? Uh, uh, uh, uh, you see...* The man is still a Kennedy. Ladies swoon as he works the room. When he reaches my mother, though, it's the other way around. Like Roger Mudd on CBS News, she leaves Ted Kennedy speechless.

"I'm from Massachusetts," she finally says. "Fall River. BMC Durfee High. Head cheerleader *and* National Honor Society."

"I never had any doubts," Kennedy says. And he stands there for another long half minute, his wide face sweating, mesmerized. He already knows he doesn't stand much chance of the nomination, but what's a primary fight against a sitting President of his own party compared to this woman, my mother, whose name he will never know?

THE VAC-HAUL

For hours we listened to it on the radio, and not once did Larry Phoebus say a word. A woman walked into a classroom of a school a couple of towns over and began shooting. She killed an eight-year-old boy and wounded three other kids. She'd also, the radio said, left homemade bombs at other schools, including a school just a few blocks from where Larry Phoebus and I were parked. I could hear the frantic sirens, like crazed, amplified mosquitoes. Now the radio said that the police confirmed that the woman had fled across the street from the school where she shot the kids and was holed up in a house with a hostage. This was in 1988, when things like this still had the capacity to shock. I was sitting there with Larry Phoebus, looking out the windshield of the truck, staring at the Chicago and Northwestern tracks, at the tall weeds that grew up between the ties, listening to all this on WBBM News-radio 780.

I was home from my first year at college. It was July. I'd wandered across that year, as I'd wandered across much else, incurious, biding my time. Waiting for what, I couldn't say. My stepfather, who was mayor of our town, found me a job in the

Streets and Sanitation Department. For a few weeks, I was proudly blue-collar. Work—who would have thought I would take it? I worked for Streets as a jackhammerer. I destroyed curbs with erotic abandon. I will make this corner handi-capped-accessible if it's my last act on earth. I wore a sweaty red bandanna. Rudimentary biceps were beginning to rise between my shoulders and elbows like small loaves. I'd be uptown, standing on the street, encircled by a little ring of pylons, smoking, and I would tell the imaginary pom-pom girls who thronged around me, I can't talk right now. Look, can't you ladies see I'm a workingman?

Then I was late three mornings in a row and the crew boss, Miguel, said, I'm taking you off Streets. You're with Larry Phoebus now.

No, Miguel, no—please—

And don't run to your dad. He knows all about it. He said to go ahead and fire you, but I figure, why not let you quit on your own?

He's not my dad.

Turn in your gloves, Hirsch. You won't need them again. Ever.

Larry Phoebus worked on the Sanitation side. He drove an enormous white truck with an enormous, bulbous hose attached to the end of it. It was called the Vac-Haul. It was rumored to have cost the taxpayers of Highland Park two mil-lion dollars. My stepfather was very proud of it. The Vac-Haul was designed to suck up major sewage backups without the need to send "manpower down the manhole," as my former

Streets partner, Steve Boland, explained it. The truck was Larry Phoebus's baby. He was long past retirement age. He'd worked for Sanitation for something like fifty years and was now refusing to leave. It was said that he didn't trust another living soul with the Vac-Haul, and when it was time for him to die, he was going to drive that two million dollars straight into Lake Michigan.

Also, Larry never spoke. It was said around the lunch table that Larry Phoebus had pretty much given up communing with the rest of the human race in the 1960s when the world, his world, everybody's world, went so haywire. Yet the precise reason for his total silence was a mystery nobody was especially interested in solving. Only Steve Boland speculated at all. He liked to hold forth in the lunchroom. Love, Boland said, what else is new under the sun? Only a woman could numb a guy like that. I hit the mute button myself for a couple of years after my first divorce. She took all my money, the house. Even then I had to sell the boat to pay her monthly. So I mean, answer me this, you're living by yourself in some dump-ass rented apartment in Highwood and you think you're going to want to chitchat?

"What the hell are you yattering about?" Miguel said.

"I'm talking about alone," Boland said. "Do any of you even know what that means?"

Larry Phoebus himself never appeared in the lunchroom. He ate in the Vac-Haul. At lunch, he'd glide the magisterial truck into its special parking place in the garage and pull out a sandwich from his jacket pocket. We'd watch him up there in his cab, slowly chewing, looking down at us but not seeming to see very much.

Being Larry Phoebus's assistant was the worst job in either division, and they usually gave it to one of the illegal Mexicans who'd come in looking for a day's work, but that day, the day I was late a third day in a row, none of those guys were around, and so I became Larry's new boy.

The Vac-Haul needed two people to operate it. One to guide the hose into the hole, the other to flick the switch in the cab.

The worst part of the worst job was that the Vac-Haul was rarely put to use. No question that it was a great monument to the progress of modern sewage engineering, but the town's system apparently functioned just fine. Yet, in order for Larry Phoebus to be paid (and for the department and the town to justify the expense), the Vac-Haul had to leave the garage. And so every morning and every afternoon, Larry Phoebus would parade the truck around town for a while and then park behind the White Hen Pantry to wait out the hours listening to the news on the radio. And so maybe to Larry Phoebus that day was no different from any other day. Maybe the voices on the radio were a little more hysterical than usual, but it all amounted to the same never-ending drone that was life outside the cab.

WBBM news time: 3:26. In Winnetka this hour, SWAT teams and hostage negotiators have descended upon the 300 block of...

Sweltering hot in the cab. Larry Phoebus never rolled the windows down and he didn't run the air conditioner, either. I listened to the old man's wheezy breathing in the stagnant air. I watched the side of his gaunt face and tried to think of something to say. Things must have been so different when you were a young kid, huh, Larry? How were things when you were young, Larry? Let's turn off the radio and talk, Larry. You and me. Tell me your life, Larry. I'll listen. Who'd you love, Larry? You must have loved somebody. Steve Boland says there's no other explanation.

Larry Phoebus watched the railroad tracks, the weeds. Finally, I got down out of the cab and went in the White Hen and bought some doughnuts, a box, an assortment. Back in the truck, I held the box out to Larry Phoebus, and in my memory, my ceaselessly lying memory, Larry Phoebus turns to me, and though he doesn't exactly speak, his eyes look at me and say, No, but thank you.

Maybe I thought the doughnuts would provide a little fellowship, break some bread, at a time like this. A time like what? What was that time like? I sat there with my doughnuts. Every once in a while I took a bite out of one and put it back in the box. I figured I'd sample the whole assortment. What the hell? I seem to remember maple frosting was a new, radical flavor then. You're dead, Larry. You would have to be long dead by now. The Vac-Haul is probably not such a marvel anymore, either. You were a man I sat next to, a man who for hours and hours I sat next to.

When I think of that time, I think of the tenacity of that man's breathing. I think of her, too. For weeks, her name was everywhere. She grew up not far from where I did. Like me, she was a suburban Jewish kid from just outside Chicago. We are legion; we hail from a place called the North Shore, a peaceful place on the bluffs of Lake Michigan. I never knew her, she was about eight or nine years older, but I did go to high school with her cousin. She—we don't say her name out loud—went to college in Madison, like my brother, like my father. She was a member of the same sorority that my grand-mother was a founding member of in 1926.

Valerie Bertinelli played her in the TV movie.

We listened to it on the radio, Larry Phoebus and me. The radio said another shot fired. The radio said SWAT teams. The radio said house surrounded.

We were still in the truck, in the parking lot, waiting out the hours before the Vac-Haul could go home to the garage, when the radio announced another shot, a lone one. The empty parking lot, the train tracks, the tall weeds growing up through the ties. I thought something should change, that at least the light should change. But it was July in the Midwest and the sun refused to sink. Only the radio voices were moving. I gripped my doughnuts. The heat in the cab rose with every breath Larry Phoebus took. The side of his motionless face. The radio said stormed the house. Was he hearing any of this? His sharp jutting chin pebbled with gray hair. A strong, ready chin. Even hiding in the parking lot, Larry Phoebus never slouched. In the event of a catastrophic sewage emergency, Larry Phoebus would be there, on the scene. Flash-flood warnings called to him in dreams. The radio said hostage in critical condition. The radio said suspect shot herself in the mouth. The guy from the White Hen came out with a huge bag of garbage and launched it, shot-put style, to the top of the already heaping Dumpster.

PART III

*In Moscow
Everything Will
Be Different*

The time I said it was only an emotional affair and you took your clothes off in front of a train. Not in front of the train as in front of the engine, in front of the side of the train. It was after eight o'clock in midsummer. The shadow of the water tower hovered over the town like an enormous bulbous spider. OTTUMWA. Amtrak was three hours late from Chicago. Freight causing delays. You waited until the train began to arrive to let me know what you thought of such idiot phrases like emotional affair. You want some fucking emotion? Always you see a train before you hear it. At first, it is only that burning headlight charging forward out of the wet haze. You didn't say anything. No unbuttoning or unzipping. Only that sudden pulling apart of your shirt and wiggling your jeans shorts off easy. Those weary passengers got a good look at you. One woman, I remember, nodded her head with what seemed an infinite amount of understanding. The body I knew so well and loved but had never seen before in public or in this vinegar light.

OTTUMWA, IOWA, 2001

ROMAN MORNING

A large flat, in the neighborhood of Via Trieste, many closed doors, room after room. We're solidly bourgeoisie, Rocco had said as he unlocked the gate. If there was a convention, we followed it. My father was a doctor before—Rocco stopped. Well, you'll see. And it was true. The first thing you noticed walking in the front door was layers of writing scrawled across the walls, in pen: smallish, purposeful writing, phone numbers, names of old friends, names of products. (In the bathroom, vertically alongside the mirror, *Nivea, Nivea, Nivea*.) But mostly they seemed to be jumbled sentences. Faulkner wrote on his walls, I said. Faulkner wasn't out of his mind, Rocco said. At least not completely. My father wanted to be a great researcher, he dreamed of making groundbreaking discoveries. The last thing he wanted was to see patients, with their ailments, their complaints, their smells. But that's what he did. And he never received the university appointment he always wanted; he was only a family doctor. After work he'd close himself up in his study for hours. His specialty he said, was childhood diseases, the mumps in particular. But it was never entirely clear to us what exactly he was trying to find. He must have thought we wouldn't have understood. A few years ago I visited my parents after my son was born, the first grandchild, and my father shuffled over to me in those paper slippers he always wore around the house, holding a fat book. Have a look, he said. It was *Who's Who*. My father wanted me to know he'd been listed in *Who's Who*. Everybody's listed in *Who's Who*. You pay a little money, they give you a little entry. My sad father. The only one who ever believed in him was my mother and this only seemed to frustrate him. It was her *job* to believe in him. What he craved was the recognition of other people. And even my mother, over the years, began to doubt him. A half century of him shutting himself in his study with his medical texts in English. In the morning, he saw patients at his office. He was a fine doctor, an excellent doctor, but there are many excellent doctors. My father wanted to stand out, to be known, and this whole place is built on this unfulfilled ambition. Always, he had to be different. Every one of his friends married Italian girls, so my father found himself a German wife. And although she spoke excellent Italian, she rarely left the house. As a child I remember her being here — always — but there was some part of her, the corner of her eye, let's say, that was somewhere else. When she finally had to put him in a home, the first thing she did was move back to Bavaria. She said she wanted to be closer to her parents' graves. Now when she visits my father, she stays in a hotel. I am supposed to be selling the place. I have to have it painted, obviously.

I think of waking up in that quiet flat, Rocco still asleep, and wandering around all those rooms laden with heavy furniture. Doors opening up into still more rooms, those walls and the chains of words, a mind trying to hold on to something, anything. But it all keeps falling. My train won't leave for another couple of hours.

EISENDRATH

The same scene as in Act I. Eight o'clock in the evening. Behind the scenes in the street there is the faintly audible sound of a concertina. There is no light.

Eisendrath finds himself early on in Act II of *Three Sisters.* He's on the stage of the New Players Community Theatre in Covington, Kentucky. It's opening night, the high-school gym. How he got here isn't important right now. Neither is the fact that Eisendrath hasn't acted since an eighth-grade production of *Little Mary Sunshine,* and even then he was only one of a chorus of five singing forest rangers. The last time he was in Kentucky was five years ago, before his life imploded. His lines, what in the fuck are his lines?

Masha Prozorova Kulygina, who is facing him, now says something incomprehensible after a long and seemingly meaningful pause.

MASHA: What noise there is in the stove right now. Not long before Father's death there was a howling in the chimney just like that. The very same!

Eisendrath is, at least he is supposed to be, the irredoubtable Aleksandr Ignatyevich Vershinin, forty-three, formerly the Lovesick Major, a man with two children and a wife who frequently, even once during the play itself, tries to poison herself just to spite you. A gallant who breezily says, *Two or three hundred years from now, the world will be inexpressibly beautiful and all this suffering will have been worth it.* In Act III, a place we will not reach tonight, Masha confesses to her sisters that she loves Vershinin for his voice, his speeches, his theorizing, his misfortunes, but even now, in Act II, Eisendrath can see this love in her eyes. The woman playing Masha is not a great actress, but she's trying, and she's not unsubtle, and she's even a little beautiful in exactly the way the three sisters are beautiful: weary, resigned, fatigued by expectation. If only they could make it back to Moscow. Everything would be different in Moscow. By day Masha is Susan Stempler and she works eighty-hour weeks in Customer Service at Bank One across the river in Cincinnati. She has yearned to act since she was a kid, and here she is — and here is Vershinin, a glib character if there ever was one, and he has suddenly and irrevocably forgotten all his lines, apparently who the hell he is, even.

Eisendrath tries looking at the scars in the wood of the stage, at the audience, which is nothing but a black muddle. He can feel the hot breath of all the people wafting on his cheeks. He stares back at her, at this Masha who is taller than he in flat shoes, who is miserably married to the jolly ignoramus Kulygin, the schoolmaster. This will be the longest moment of his life, not because time stops, but because it continues to stomp forward and onward like the triple-named soldiers of Vershinin's own platoon, who pound through the back rooms of this play. Eisendrath's fear is so palpable at this point it could almost be mistaken for drama. A man in one of the back rows begins to cough ravenously, and his boomings echo as if the entire gym is at the bottom of some canyon, and still Masha locks her exhausted, sorrowful eyes on Eisendrath, eyes that of course are also Susan Stempler's, begging him to say something, anything, anything at all, *just move your lips.* We're about to move from glitch to fiasco. How fast we can sink. Eisendrath looks down at his uniform as if there's a clue in the olive jacket the volunteer costume designer (also playing the crone Anfisa) picked up at the army surplus. Vershinin has a few medals, not many. This is to show that in spite of his many years of loyal military service, he's never been much for valor. The Lovesick Major's head is too much in the clouds. Eisendrath looks around at the set, at the drawing room, at the old but solid, not yet ratty furniture. Weird. It's all vaguely familiar. And though there's no chance whatsoever that his lines are lodged somewhere in his brain—Eisendrath is not even certain he's ever even read this play—he almost feels like settling down, right here in this little gymnasium. Sweat and tears course down Susan Stempler's cheeks, and her eyes, desperate now—this, the one thing I've ever wanted. Can't you speak at all?

Panic rises in the wings and then a voice, shouting disguised as a whisper:

WINGS: Are you superstitious?
VERSHININ: Are you superstitious?
MASHA: Yes, I am superstitious.
WINGS: That's strange. *(Pause.)* You're a splendid,
    wonderful woman, splendid, wonderful. It's dark in
    here and I can see your eyes shining.

VERSHININ: That's strange —

(Masha shoves her hand in Eisendrath's face, and so he kisses it, Susan's hand. It tastes of sweat and Jergen's.)

VERSHININ: You're a splendid, winderful woman. It's dark and I can hear your eyes shining.

(Masha walks over to the other side of the stage, plops in a chair, crosses her feet.)

MASHA: It's lighter over here.

Eisendrath tries to move closer to the light, but he can't, his feet won't budge, and perhaps thirty seconds pass, maybe even a minute, and he does not hear the wings begging, nearly shrieking now —

WINGS: I love you, I love you...

VERSHININ:

MASHA: When you talk to me like this, for some reason I laugh, though I am frightened. Please don't say it again...Say it again. Go ahead, I don't care. *(Covers her eyes with her hands.)*

WINGS: I love your eyes, I love the way you move...

VERSHININ:

MASHA: Say it! I don't care! Say it!

VERSHININ: A play is a fixed planet, and Eisendrath has fallen off by now. But even this doesn't matter anymore. Love? How would he know it if he saw it? He'd stroke Susan Stempler's now drenched face if he could reach her, if he could ever reach her.

WOMAN IN A DUBROVNIK CAFÉ

Do you remember her? It was sunny. Her hair was pulled back and sunglasses rode the top of her head like another pair of darkened eyes. She had white cream on her face. She talked about her father, her mother, her tabby cats, her white-bearded cats, her Siamese. She said she was afraid in London now.

"I'm not bigot, but when it gets to the point, you don't see a white face for blocks —" She stopped abruptly and reached for your hand. "Such exquisite hands. Do you play piano? My father played beautifully. He was English. Mother was a Serb. Father met her while looking for oil near Novi Sad. He left her when I was ten. Mother didn't kill herself right away. She let a reasonable amount of time pass. We lived in Shrewsbury then. I went with father to the funeral. He said *Goodbye, Netty* to the casket and then shoveled dirt and rocks on it. She has a large headstone. Mother's family were very cosmopolitan Jews. They read the paper on Saturdays, drove. Hard to believe now when you read what barbarians the Serbs are. Tony Blair's dumber than toast. And your Clinton's truly disgusting. My cousin Anna a barbarian! If you could see her in the little dresses she used to make. I just came from Novi Sad. They're walking around like they're already dead, waiting for more bombs to drop. Yes, there are still some Jews left in Yugoslavia. Would you like a chocolate? My father didn't hate my mother, he just, well, tired of her, and that's a crime really, because it's laziness. A man who played Bach like that whispering goodbye under his breath at her grave like she was going somewhere on a train. Would you like more coffee? The waiter knows I'm Serb — that's why he ignores us. He can hear it in my accent. I really should speak English here. I'm sorry. I'm sorry for so much. Isn't it funny to be so sorry for things? You two are quite nice. Normally, I loathe Americans. You know, my brother moved to someplace called Rockville in Washington, D.C., and I tell him over e-mail that I'll visit him over my dead body, and let me tell you, he won't come mutter over my grave, because I've left instructions — cremation within twenty-four hours of my demise. My lawyer has the papers. They're fully executed. I'll be taking up no more space here after I'm gone. Things are crowded enough as it is. I say, when it's over, let the flames announce it. Bring me to the fire — don't you agree? — the fire."

REVEREND HRNCIRIK RECEIVES AN
AIRMAIL PACKAGE
Brno, Czechoslovakia, 1963

A slant of rain against the one small window. As there was rain those three days she was here and he had imagined her clothes strewn across this little office. Why lie? There were moments when his lust made it difficult to breathe. The thing he wanted most was her mouth. He thinks of how it scowled at him. Yet her eyes claimed the opposite. There was kindness in them, a kind of dampened kindness. As though her eyes were battling with her mouth over which face to show him. What is more advantageous, ferocity or gentleness? He remembers wondering whether this struggle stretched into other regions. Imagined her torso white, its lower half a gorgeous hellfire of blue and orange.

She worked with an international charitable organization of some sort. The UNESCO office in Prague had arranged for her visit to Brno to facilitate "cross-cultural exchange," which was a permissible, if dubious, exercise in the eyes of the authorities. She was an American living in Geneva. He'd learned

English in London during the war. Over the course of two days, they had had long talks in this office, talks she thought were illicit, and in a way they were. Any candid conversation with someone from the West carried some risks, but this was years before the Soviet invasion and Barbara Hoffman's questions were so quaint—*Reverend, is it true they've outlawed your God?*—that they couldn't possibly have attracted the attention of anyone but the most bored of informants. Barbara Hoffman was thrilled danger lurked and so chattered on, at times looking furtively from under her shaggy eyebrows at the window ledge, as though she expected, any moment, the ghost of Stalin's fur hat to rise above the sill.

He interrupted. "My God? I beg your pardon, Mrs. Hoffman. What about yours?"

"Is *He* still here? I thought he was long gone. I no longer believe. I suppose I used to, must have outgrown it. Two days ago, I met with a couple of rabbis in Prague and felt nothing. Isn't that sad? All those years of *being* something and I come back here to what—the old country?—and I can't muster any kinship. They just looked like poor, tattered souls, not family."

"There are so few Jews left, of course."

"All the more reason I should have been moved, no?"

"What moves us is a complicated question."

"I'm not making you uncomfortable, Reverend, am I?"

He'd waved her away with a doorlike swing of his small, hairless hand. A short, gregarious woman in white heels. She sat across this very desk and watched herself through his eyes. She saw a bold woman willing to reach across the great chasm to provide aid and comfort to a poor Lutheran pastor in poor, oppressed Czechoslovakia. So he told her stories, some of them even true, detailing the hardships of running a church in such times. The limitations on what services he could offer, the constantly changing and arbitrary laws, the threat of spies, the disastrous plumbing in the rectory. To get a decent plumber to come to a church you have to know someone in the Politburo! And she'd listened to his boastful anecdotes about the whispering, nudging, and *yes, I've had to do a bit of bribing here and there.* He'd spread his arms wide, not exactly knowing why, but trying in his way to say, I embrace not only the misery of myself and my people but of mankind! "Of course," he'd said quietly, "I'm insignificant."

A good woman, perhaps not yet fifty, trolling around for something good to do in this world, and she'd landed, of all places, in this office. She was going to ship him a new mimeograph machine, paper, books, office supplies. Even a boxload of Bibles in Czech. At one point in the last hour of the second day, there was a lull in their conversation. Barbara Hoffman didn't like lulls. But this particular moment she didn't fill it; instead, she waited. Then she blurted out so harshly it was as though she'd stomped on his foot:

"I was married for two weeks."

"Two weeks?"

"Felt like a hell of a long time. At the end of the second week—we were still on our honeymoon in Ireland—he turned to me and said, 'Well?' And I said, 'Well, what?' For the life of the man he couldn't think of anything else to say."

Reverend Hrncirik couldn't either. He gaped at her.

"And it didn't rain in Ireland. The entire time I kept waiting. You never married?"

12/14/63

My dear Reverend Hrncirik,

Don't think I have forgotten the happy days I spent in Brno. I'm sending along to you Alan Paton's second novel. I wouldn't say that it is as groundbreaking as the first; nonetheless, Paton continues to expose. This one is about a delicious creature called the Immorality Act, which prohibits contact of a carnal nature between the races. Contact of a carnal nature! Can you imagine the bureaucrat that came up with that particular phraseology?

The book is a paperback. On the front it says, "For the considerable audience that hailed *Cry, the Beloved Country* as a literary and popular masterpiece, Alan Paton has produced another novel of similar beauty, equal power, and even greater readability — *The Denver Post*." Denver! Americans! Even their books are advertisements. To be barked at like that while you are trying to read. This one is called *Too Late the Phalarope*. He looks up phalarope in his English dictionary: *Kinds of small, wading and swimming birds known for their timidity.* He lays the book aside and straightens some papers on his desk. He'd planned to write some letters and to finish a report before Barbara Hoffman returned. And make no mistake, a letter is a return. Three sentences of one letter and the salutation of another — he crumples both. He picks up hers again and rubs the tissue-thin paper between his fingers. He raises it to his nose as if it might carry her scent. It smells faintly of dust. They'd gotten to talking about books. She'd loaned him one she'd just finished, a book with such a beautiful title, Barbara Hoffman had said, it made her want to plant it in a garden. He'd read *Cry, the Beloved Country* in one sleepless night, in a fever. In a bleary—and theatrical—

Moment at 4 a.m., he'd knelt and kissed the book. How else to honor such a man, such a pastor, as this black Father Kumalo? Reverend Hrncirik had been so shamed that the next day he'd babbled at Barbara Hoffman like a fool...*Unless all the churches, mine, the Episcopalians, my Lord, even the Catholics, everybody, regain consciousness"*— He'd stopped himself and slapped the book on the table. *"Ah, but what's the incentive for this? Churches sleep now, as we slept before. Ask your rabbis in Prague. For every Bonhoeffer there's a thousand men like me."* He gazed around his tiny office, but he was really looking beyond it, at the crumbling altar of his church, at the weary streets of his city, at his people walking, bundled.

He talked on, ignoring her protests. *"And this Father Kumalo? He's enough to make you abandon forgiveness as any sort of answer. When you see it only twisted, increasing paralysis. They heap tribulation. He forgives. They heap. He forgives. It isn't supposed to work like this."*

"An old story," Barbara Hoffman said.

Reverend Hrncirik laughed. "But remember, even Christ chased the moneychangers. That old man? He's almost monstrous in his patience. No anger, only love, as his son hangs."

"What are you suggesting, Reverend?"

"I don't know."

"That forgiveness doesn't always work?"

"Keep it between us."

Barbara Hoffman laughed with her eyes. "In this sense, I agree with you. Perhaps the only answer in a place like South Africa is brute force." She paused. But—the West, with our obsession with Communism. We only have the capacity to understand one evil at a time. Besides, the South Africans are such good capitalists."

Ah, Communism! He smiled and wrapped his throat with both hands, mock strangling.

Now Barbara Hoffman didn't laugh. She only looked at him, Why haven't you touched me, Reverend Hrncirik? Why haven't you reached across your desk and touched me?

They both listened to the rain.

I heard Paton speak in Belgium in November. He said he had little hope for a peaceful solution in South Africa. Perhaps he is coming around to facing the inevitable. You may have heard that after his last trip abroad, his passport was seized by his government and he is no longer permitted to leave the country. A quiet man, but a powerful one. Please tell me all your news and

On the evening of the second night she'd asked him to her hotel room for some chocolate. "Swiss." She laughed. "I smuggled it over the border." And he declined with a bow, making it clear there was nothing wrong with the invitation in an academic sense—it wasn't as though he was celibate, he'd had other women over the years—but he wouldn't accept her offer, anyway. What was it he wanted to punish her for? For being as lonely as he was? He remembers feeling simply tired, or rather, he remembers that he had an expectation of being tired later. I'm exhaustible, he thought. I am a man whom things exhaust before they've even happened.

Now, this afternoon, he thinks, I could have listened to her

voice. I could have just watched her lips move. He was a man
who nursed all the proper notions, beginning with his bedrock
belief that to restrict belief is to oppress God and that such blas-
phemy is fathomless. But his actions, *his actions*, amounted to
begging help from plumbers and electricians. He thinks of
Father Kumalo hiking up the mountain, that old man feeling
his way in the dark with a stick. There are no small heroes. He
looks around his office at the stacks of requisition forms, at the
old bronze clock, at one of his gloves lying on the floor. He
exists. This church exists. Will it ever be enough? He drums his
fingers on the book. Who's the timid bird? He thinks of the
uselessness of being a man people don't want to even silence,
much less kill. He laughs at how beyond him it all is. A man
without the courage to love, where would he find the courage to
stand up? Against what? A shadow darkens the cloudy glass of
his door window. Slowly, like a much older man than he is, he
rises. His parishioners always lurk like that. Always, they hover
in the corridor. Why won't they knock? He sits back down. He
won't open it. Wait, whoever you are, wait. Let you wait. Let the
old widows wait. Let the man from Pardubice with the sick
daughter wait. Let Jesus himself wait, wait for him, Reverend
Ota Hrncirik. He slumps in his chair, allows her image to tun-
nel into his stomach, sink down his legs. He'd gone back to his
room that night and masturbated slowly, with the light on. He
fingers the soiled handkerchief in his pocket and wants to do it
again now, even almost gently, like he did that night. Not with
that impatience at the door, not with this book on the desk, not
with her letter silently—what? Asking? Goading? Forgiving?

MILLARD'S BEACH, 1984

Call these the meditations of an overweight junior life-guard watching an empty lake, up in this chair lording over nobody. The last swimmer gave it up hours ago, late-afternoon September, the day gray and lingering. The lake is nearly motionless. The waves curdle up the shore like frosting. He thinks of what it might be like to actually save someone. Guard, my child. Oh, guard, my daughter, oh, guard, do something, do something — and so, stiffen the sinews, summon the blood, dishonor not your mothers. Into the breach he cata-pults, out past the buoys designating the authorized swimming area, and executes the Lost Buddy Drill, except this time it's for real. He dives down, down, counting 1, 2, 3, 4, 5, 6, and he feels his way in the dark water, across the smooth, ridged bot-tom of the lake, and searches for an obstruction, the soft inert body of the newly drowned. Come up, breathe. Do it again, hero, count 1, 2, 3, 4, 5, 6, and all he wants is to feel flesh, all he wants is to break the surface with the booty, haul in the girl alive — alert the media — as people, his people, watch from the beach. Hail the chubby Adonis. No one will ever drown on his watch. This job and—how much else?—is one long unrescue. He's in charge of the blind sand, of the lake, his lake, now churning, now seething, as the wind picks up, as the gray day lingers.

DENNY COUGHLIN: IN MEMORY

Things were good for a while. A team made up of guys from Southie would play a team made up of guys from Charlestown—with a couple first-degree lifers from Chelsea or Malden thrown in to make things even up. Every Tuesday and Thursday afternoon. Can't you see Pinkhands Salerno? Nursing his eye with a frozen sausage and shouting from the sidelines, "Fuckers, this show's gotta go on!" Like we were putting on *Guys and Dolls,* opening night, on Broadway.

This place used to be called just Walpole, but the people of Walpole got tired of being known only as the town with the prison, until the state of Massachusetts changed the gulag's name to Cedar Junction, a mythical place, an intersection of horrors just off Route 47 North. Turn right at the Dairy Delight and keep going a mile and a half. Paint scabbed, looks like an abandoned factory but for the layers of razor wire loop-di-looped, glistening sliver in the sun, and the warning signs and the guard towers and the machine gunners.

Denny Coughlin made the rules, and Salerno, his most faithful lieutenant, carried them out with the zeal of a convert. Denny Coughlin. Good old Boston Irish from an old Southie family. Some of the sons went into the racket, others into politics. When his brother Len got hitched, Mike Dukakis gave the bride away. Denny, though, was in the crime branch, and back then—he'd be the first to admit it—he was a few clowns short of a circus. He got lugged on a murder two for busting a former associate in the head with a tire iron behind the Shell station on Columbus Boulevard. Denny pled to manslaughter and landed twelve to fourteen at Walpole, where he rose to his true calling, prison floor hockey.

The game had two basic rules:

Rule 1: *No injuries.* If you got hurt enough so that you couldn't play, you dragged yourself off to the sidelines, stuffed your elbow back in the socket or got a towel to stanch whatever was bleeding. But you were forbidden to go to the choke. The rule came about because Sergeant Whosafuck said the game was getting too expensive after Rent Meelhan got blunked by Fabain and Joey Norris and had to be carried off, blood gushing from his eyes, on a stretcher. Spent a week in the choke with five broken ribs and a knob on his head big as Uranus. Finally they had to send him to a real hospital. So Whosafuck said, "Next time somebody goes down like that, that'll be it, and you useless hogs will suck each other's dicks while the blacks get double gym time for basketball."

"Sergeant Whosafuck, must you be so vulgar?" Salerno asked. "Think of the tender ears. We've got juveniles here tried as adults."

"Hustoff, Salerno. Hustoff. It's Slovenian."

And so Coughlin decreed it: "The days of wine and pain are over." Nobody would get hurt again—ever. Salerno was a trustee. He'd steal the frozen meat from the kitchen that we'd use for icepacks.

Rule 2, which was around before we needed Rule 1, was straightforward also: *The puck is always live.* No time-outs. Constant action. The game never stopped unless the puck went under the equipment cage on the far side of the gym. When this happened, one of the screws would have to get up off his lolling ass and open the metal gate to retrieve the puck. Now, the important thing to understand here was that the puck remained live even when it went under the wooden bench the officers sat on during games. The drill was that the screws covering the gym — usually Morton and Salazar — would leap up whenever the puck went under the bench so that the guys could fight over the puck until somebody dug it out. The screws — at least Morton and Salazar — knew the deal. Plus, they got a kick out of seeing us beat the living crap out of each other up close. So when the puck went under the bench (about three times a game), they ran for the hills.

(The only other rule, so minor it didn't need a number, was that blacks didn't play floor hockey. But this was less a rule than the simple fact that the blacks, according to Coughlin, were scared pissless to play the barbarians. *Same reason they don't come to Southie. We're big and white and hairy, baby!*)

Nobody ever got hurt, nobody went to the choke. So maybe it was surprising that it was Rule 2 that caused Whosafuck to finally ban hockey, after all the trouble we went through to enforce Rule 1.

It was a tight game, only four minutes left before count call. Charlestown up by one. Coughlin was having an off day; he hadn't scored. For a big man he had a strange grace as he went after the puck. He moved with this real fluid motion, as if he really was on ice skates. I played for Southie, defense. I'm not that aggressive a guy. I'm in here on a murder one, crime of passion, my lawyer called it. And it was love, that much is true, but I'm not making excuses — anyway, too long a story. In the gym, I rarely moved much. I'm decently sized myself, and mostly I just stood there in front of our goal like those cement pots they use to block off a street. Sometimes my head wouldn't even be that much in the game because I'd be too busy watching Coughlin. There isn't any other way to say it. Out there on the floor he wasn't inside, he was somewhere else. And he'd thread through a bunch of guys, twirl like a ballerina, and come out with the puck like it was glued to his stick. It was a beautiful thing to watch. Losing brought out the artist in him. He never wanted to crush Charlestown; he always wanted them to believe they could beat us. Coughlin always said you had to give Charlestown some reason to believe. Otherwise, why would they ever play?

That day I think Coughlin may have pulled something, because he was favoring his left side a bit, but as soon as he heard the first warning bell, five minutes to count, his body seemed to forget about it and he got the old hunger back. But Charlestown had some strong players and they were hanging in there; most of them dropped back to defend. They kept deflecting Coughlin's shots — with not only their sticks but their shoes, their elbows, their necks, their teeth. It was getting bloody down there on their side of the gym. Charlestown was smelling it. And Coughlin, with only about two or minutes to go, had decided enough was enough —

Another shot ricocheted off the goal, and this time the puck went under the officers' bench. And, see, that day a brand-new screw was down in the gym and he didn't know the rules. Morton, the lazy fuck, didn't bother to tell him. Salazar would have told him. Salazar would have showed him the ropes. But Morton, never. It would have taken too much energy to open his mouth and say, Hey, listen, rook, when the puck goes under the bench, they'll kill you if you don't get out of the way, okay? What would it have taken? And so of course, when it happened, the twenty-year-old puny rookie screw didn't have any sense. Even though Morton was practically in New Hampshire when that puck slid under the bench that day. But the kid didn't move. I'm a guard, the kid thinking, I'm wearing a uniform. I have to move for these Neanderthals? Two hundred fifty-five pounds of Denny Coughlin barreling his way, and the kid sits there on a picnic. Coughlin couldn't stop, and he popped the kid so hard his head mulched against the concrete wall like a kicked-in pumpkin. It was bad. Morton, who knew damn well Coughlin was only going for the puck, fucked him anyway. That's your Rule 3: They will always fuck us anyway. He got on his radio and called in an emergency B single assault on an officer. It didn't take more than sixty seconds for Whosafuck to burst in with six helmeted Nazi lunatics from the Special Operations Response Team, plastic shields in one hand, wombats in the other. And the SORTs went right for Coughlin. But hear this, Coughlin, even on the floor, even getting his teeth kicked in by the toes of the SORT screws' boots—the man still spoke up for the game, for us:

"Puck's always live. Puck's only dead when it goes in the cage!"

And when they dragged him away by his pits and he was

nearly unconscious, his blood across the gym floor, he kept sputtering that he didn't need to go to the choke, that he was fine, absolutely fucking fine.

Salerno told us what happened after. He had contacts in the choke. They couldn't save him, so they had him medivaced to Mass General. But that was only covering their asses. Denny Coughlin was brain dead before he rose up from Cedar Junction.

A Chinese restaurant in a strip mall off I-495 in Lawrence, Massachusetts, just across the road from the huge, white, boxlike Showcase Cinemas. Seitz looked out the window and watched the cars leaving the parking lot. The restaurant was dark. Each table had its own light, a small round bulb behind a red shade. Seitz thought: Our own sad moon. He listened to two ladies chat in the next booth.

"No kidding. Every day she goes home to make dinner for a man who's been dead seventeen years. She says he lives in the radiator."

"Like my cousin Aurelia, long conversations with her cat. She talks and talks and then pauses while she listens to the cat."

His food arrived. Seitz ate slowly, as was his habit. He always looked closely at each bite of food before he put it in his mouth. There was a commotion. The waiter and the manager ran back and forth between the kitchen and the men's room, both of which were in the back of the restaurant. They tried not to shout. A hushed panicked way of whispering. Ten or so minutes later, the police arrived, followed immediately by the paramedics. The cops asked everybody, seven people in total, a family of four, the two ladies, himself, if they would please step outside and wait to be questioned. Bring your coats, please. There was one table with a plate of half-eaten food and a full beer but no diner.

Out on the sidewalk one of the ladies said, "See, Marion, something's always happening. Last week, the flat tire and running into Cindy Donatello after how long?"

Seitz and the waiter leaned against a parked car and watched more cops arrive. These upper-level cops, or so Seitz imagined that's what they were, moved languidly, confidently, like they did on television. He wondered if they sat around all day waiting for things like this, like actors in their dressing rooms.

"Not that cold," the waiter said.

"Actually not," Seitz said. "Unseasonable."

The waiter assured him that what had happened had nothing to do with the food. "I'm not saying it's especially great," the waiter said.

"What happened?"

"Guy got whacked in the men's room."

"Tonight?"

"Only once or twice in the head," the waiter said. "But enough."

"Dead?"

"Totally."

"And nobody heard?"

"Hand drier was on. The thing sounds like a plane landing."

A cop came up to Seitz. "You a patron?"

"Patron?"

"Could I ask you a few questions?"

The cop led him to one of the squad cars. They stood by the hood. The sun was down, but the parking lot lights remained bright. The squad car was still running, which added to the sense of excitement. Seitz explained that he'd been on his way home from a sales call in Kittery, Maine, when he'd gotten hungry. He'd never been to the place before, just passing by. Hadn't heard a thing.

"What do you sell?"

"Hardware."

"Wrenches, hammers?"

"Computer hardware."

"Oh, right, right. What's your name?"

"Donald Seitz."

"And your address, Mr. Seitz?"

"129 Florence Street. Malden, Mass. 02148."

All Seitz knew about Lawrence was what he read in the papers, that it was a city on fire. This was in 1995, and Lawrence was the arson capital of the country. Building by building, block by block, they were burning the old mill town down. Seitz thought of waking up in the night and seeing the sunrise glow at the wrong time of day. He could see the attraction, almost the love you had to have of old buildings, these red-brick New England monstrosities, to want to see them turned to ash. Think of the heat you need to burn brick. Of course, out here by the highway, you couldn't see the city at all. Out here wasn't Lawrence or anywhere really. He thought of the dead man. He thought of his unfinished plate of food.

The manager apologized to everyone personally and

handed out coupons. The family and the two ladies walked to their cars. Then Seitz, too, left for home.

Murders weren't uncommon in Lawrence, but they weren't an epidemic, either. This one wouldn't have made the Boston press had it not been for the novel way the man had been killed. Slaughtered like a veal calf in a bathroom stall during business hours. The metro section of the *Boston Herald* ran the story for a couple of days. After that there wasn't anything more to say. The bathroom window was found open. Police concluded that the killer must have come in and out the window. The murdered man was named Patrick Laplante. Unemployed, the *Herald* said, long history of drug-related arrests.

Seitz drove the forty miles back to the restaurant a week later. He was a man who redeemed coupons. Why not? It's like money in your pocket. A few days later, he drove up again, though he had no business in Kittery or anywhere else north of Boston. At first the waiter and the manager, Mr. Lee (who turned out to be the owner), said they knew nothing more about the Laplante murder than he did. But after a while they started telling him things. The waiter said there was no lack of suspects.

"One detective told me that he was thinking of putting up a wanted poster offering a reward for anybody who didn't have a reason to off Patrick Laplante. He was a runner, a little old for it. He never advanced beyond street level distribution. The word is he was skimming more than an acceptable amount off the top. Both the other runners and the chiefs wanted him over with."

Mr. Lee told him about the new policy. The door to the men's room was to remain open at all times. No exceptions. It made things awkward, but what choice did he have? He also had the hand drier dismantled and brought back paper towels. "Supposed to save me money," Mr. Lee said. "Damn thing ruins me."

Seitz became a regular customer. He'd never been a regular before. With it came a kind of belonging he'd never craved, yet he found it wasn't unpleasant. The waiter brought him a Sprite and a lemon without his asking. They must have thought he was an investigative reporter or a private investigator of some sort, a fiction he didn't discourage by taking notes on cocktail napkins. Seitz never ventured into Lawrence itself. The restaurant and the land around it were enough. Enough for what? He wasn't entirely sure. Looking out the window, Seitz thought about what used to be here. Woods? After that, farmland? That's the way he always understood it, but how could anybody tell? The grass along the interstate was well watered, but who ever walked on it? Still, you couldn't act like this place didn't exist. Hadn't something happened here, too, the ultimate thing?

Donald Seitz was a bachelor who in ten years had been with three different women, one of whom he loved. She was married when they met. She left her husband for him. Seeing how easy that was, she left Seitz a few months later. He'd always had a talent for not being lonely. He thought vaguely of his childhood, how his desire to be alone unnerved people. His mother once took him to a doctor about it. In particular, Seitz had always preferred to eat alone, at home. The Laplante murder changed this in a way that, again, he couldn't quite explain. He found himself more and more intrigued by eating alone in public. He marveled at all the things he'd been missing. Think of all that can be stuffed out, irrevocably, while you fumble through your mu shu pork with plastic chopsticks.

Four months later Seitz was sitting in what had become his booth. A Tuesday night, around 8:30. In his reflection in the window he watched how the soft skin beneath his jaw tightened as he chewed, transforming his face into someone he'd never seen before. The waiter approached. Seitz smiled.

"Mind if I sit?"

"Of course not." Seitz shoved his plate away.

"No, keep eating."

The waiter wasn't Chinese. He liked to show off the few words in Cantonese that Mrs. Lee, the cook, had taught him. The waiter's eyes were droopy and his skin was pale in spots, red with pimples in others. Seitz took his pen out of his jacket pocket and uncapped it.

"I'd rather you not write this."

"Not a problem."

Seitz glanced up at Mr. Lee, who was watching them from his post behind the bar, a towel over his shoulder. He and Mrs. Lee often argued. They always tried to keep their voices down, but eventually their voices would reach such high notes their fights became operatic. Something told Seitz that whatever made them so excited never had anything to do with the restaurant. Possibility here as well, in the arguments other people have that we'll never know the origins of or even understand. How much drama lost?

He smiled again at the waiter. "Call me all-ears," Seitz said.

The waiter leaned forward. "It's about that night—Laplante."

"Yes."

"I compromised the scene."

"What do you mean?"

The waiter put both hands on the table and edged even closer. In the red moonish light, his face didn't look as young as it did from farther away. He always looked twenty, twenty-five, but right now he could have been ten years older. "I moved the body—just a little—but who knows? Maybe I wrecked the whole investigation. All I did was tug his foot and pull him off the seat. Any idiot could see he was dead. He hardly had a mouth or nose left to breathe out of. The guy really got clocked. I just wanted to give him some dignity."

"Sounds like you did him a good turn, a human thing."

"But with all this O.J. stuff, L.A.P.D. and contamination and all that, I just worry—"

"From what I understand," Seitz said, "these cops couldn't have found the killer if he left a trail of egg rolls to his house," Seitz said. "What would a few inches matter in an investigation like this?"

The waiter laughed, but his eyes moistened. Tears? "You don't believe me."

"Why wouldn't I believe you?"

The large, pimpled face stared. Mr. Lee coughed. A couple were waiting to place their order. The waiter slid out of the booth. Seitz went to the men's room and poked around, tried to feel something. What? An absence? The place was nothing but clean.

That night he went to a late movie at the Showcase. A comedy, a love story. Seitz was one of the few people in the audience. He watched the silhouettes of solitary heads in the darkness. He'd never been much of a moviegoer, too much noise and commotion. And they'd always taken him too far away. It would take hours to adjust sometimes. After, he walked to his car and turned the key, but rather than unlocking the door, he locked it. *I forgot to lock it?* Maybe it was the movie, the surging out the exit door into the night, even a movie like this, a movie already half forgotten. He felt almost giddy. There was a tingling in his feet, his toes. He turned the key the other way and got in the car. After a few minutes of stillness, he adjusted the rearview and, in the great brightness of the overhead lights, met another pair of eyes.

"I'm not a reporter," Seitz said.

"I know," the waiter said.

"I'm not anybody."

"I know."

"Only curious."

"Yes."

Seitz looked out at the few scattered cars remaining in the vast parking lot. It looked like an emptied harbor. Tomorrow all the cars would be back.

LUBYANKA PRISON, MOSCOW, 1940

They beat him with the sawed-off legs of a chair until he admitted to being an agent of the French intelligence services. To his interrogators, Babel wrote, "If you are fundamentally flawed, then perfect this flaw in yourself and raise it to the level of art." Did they have any idea what he was trying to say? What was he trying to say? His trial lasted twenty minutes. Nothing was especially comic about any of it, but he of all people thought he should be able to find something. Will this be my last failure? Tragedy is underdeveloped comedy. An Irishman said that. Of the two guards escorting him to the place against a shiny white wall—it must be someone's job to clean it—he noticed the smaller one to his right, his waggly beard and his breath like sweetly rotting pears. Of the guard on his left, he noted only that he was more ape than man, which struck him as an uninspiring observation. His own feet, he noticed them also. One was very cold and one seemed to be on fire. The guard on his left, the big one—Babel imagines his wife's small, chapped hands. The guard on the left will rub them tonight, the sad nooks between his wife's dry fingers. This ape. She'll ask: And today? What happened today? And he'll say, Nothing much. A little Jew in glasses, twelve or so others. Come closer, won't you ever come closer?

WAUKEGAN STORY

She completed the forms and submitted them, along with a thick sheaf of notarized documentation. Long hours of doing what she had always done followed. Days of the same. Work: cleaning, cooking, marketing, washing, reading, teaching, correcting, preparing lessons. But really what Maritsa was doing was waiting, so even what was the same took longer now. One day she burned her maps in the oven, watched them ignite through the greasy little window. Still, she was waiting. Then the idea of hoping (because what is hoping if it isn't waiting?) became so abruptly foreign it scared her. She didn't need it anymore. The embassy of the United States had sent her a stamped paper.

Maritsa used to place her hands over America. Even with her fingers spread, she couldn't cover it all. Michigan's flat hat, Florida's backward chicken leg. California always longer than her own thumb.

She took her seven-year-old, Damyan, and renamed him Danny, although she insisted that his name would always be Damyan. He didn't mind. SWAT teams and Chicago Bears, the boy couldn't get enough. Her husband, Lyubomir, stayed behind in Sophia. He was a doctor and he had to close his affairs as well as transfer their tiny, despised flat. Of course, he wasn't going to be a doctor any more than she was going to be the schoolteacher she had spent the last twelve years of her life waking up and being. And what are they going to think of me there, my English being so atrocious? They'll think I'm illiterate, a moron.

"And Damyan? You'll steal his chance?"

"Don't hide behind the boy. It's you—"

So she left Lyubomir, and for months, the two of them sent letters back and forth across the ocean. In one letter, his pen ripped through the paper. He wrote that he had become a man with a wife who insisted the only way to leave a flat she hated was to move to America! Maritsa replied: *It isn't the flat, it's everything. It's the neighbors, it's the Dancescus flushing, it's the snoring, it's Razvan and Sabina's fucking we have to listen to. Can't you understand that people shouldn't have to live like this—especially now?* And always, Damyan. The unimaginable opportunity. Damyan the American! What lies! *And I'm a man who let it happen! They laugh at me, don't you see, Maritsa? They're all laughing.*

And some nights he'd wake her up just before dawn, a call they couldn't afford, and pant into the phone like an exhausted horse.

When she felt confident enough with her spoken English (she'd studied it for years, but talking to Americans was another matter altogether), she finally told the kind, stubby-fingered man at the gas station grocery who she was and what she was doing here. He spat laughter, not cruelly, only in shock: *A refugee? To Waukegan? This armpit? Come on, love, sell me something else.*

Well, not a refugee in a technical sense, but she didn't want to explain her classification and the label made it easier. She'd won a lottery and the INS placement office in Washington, D.C., had found her an apartment in what was left of this city on Lake Michigan, too far from Chicago to say she lived in Chicago.

She got a job with a maid service. Every morning she and three other women were driven in a van to clean houses in Lake Forest. Lake Forest! Now here was America! Her first morning in the van, another girl, a Jamaican, had nudged her and said, "You won't believe me."

"What?"

"The women, they clean the houses before we get there."

"What?"

"Not a joke. They clean like lunatics, these woman. Oh, you'll scrub their crap inside the toilet bowls, yes, but most of the work is already done before you walk in the house with the bucket."

Cleaning for the cleaning ladies. Maritsa found this preposterous lie to be absolutely true. So it wasn't the work that was difficult. It was only that these houses, houses as big as banks she roamed around with her tank-sized vacuum cleaner, sapped her energy in other, less definable ways. It was a kind of fatigue. She'd never imagined that proximity to wealth, unfathomable wealth, could make her so weary. She wouldn't even want it anymore.

English classes were held Tuesday and Thursday nights at the local grammar school. She sat squeezed, her knees jammed against the bottom of a tiny desk, and repeated after the teacher, whose name was Gilda Petrocelli. Not Mrs. Petrocelli or even Mrs. Gilda, only Gilda, and she had fat pink cheeks that made her look like a talking porcelain doll. She also had a husband who kept constant watch, prowling outside class, stalking the little halls like a giant in squeaky shoes. Often Gilda's husband stuck his face in the narrow, crisscrossed wire window and breathed until it fogged. It was hard to tell if the husband's problem was anger or sorrow or fear. Gilda had told the class that before she began teaching Advanced ESL, she'd been a librarian. But that's all in the past now, she said. She said it like all that cataloguing and shelving had been like fighting in some forgotten war. And maybe it had been. Teaching school had certainly been like that. Those terrible dangling feet, every morning those pairs of relentlessly staring eyes. Gilda was particularly concerned about pronunciation. She always spent the last five minutes simply saying whatever words came to her, in alphabetical order. Pronunciation holds the key, she'd say, grinning and holding up a cardboard cutout with a drawing of an old-fashioned skate key, to successful integration. These are words you know, but you must master how they *sound*. She spoke slowly, enunciating every syllable, directing them to watch her mouth.

Appetite. Butcher. Curriculum. Despondent. Evaporate.

At night she'd coo to her sleeping Damyan, but really more to herself, that where you are is in your mind, that it's got nothing to do with maps. That if you aren't in Waukegan in your mind, you aren't there. Do you hear me, little man? This isn't Waukegan, it's the Horn of Plenty...

October and she'd walk the wet streets to the gas station grocery for sliced cheese and a magazine. She'd look at the potholes full of oily water and the broken windows of the abandoned paint factory that stretched three city blocks. The buildings of Sophia were beautiful in their corruption; headless, handless statues gazed down from countless ledges. Her city was streets of crumble and scaffolds. True, there were newer buildings in Sophia, cheap flimsy apartment blocks built in a day and a half, like the box she'd moved into after she got married, but she didn't think of these when she thought of the architecture of home. In Waukegan, the buildings were not new and not old, and no one bothered to say anything about them one way or the other. They'd been built to endure and then were just left.

The man at the gas station told her that the big boats still call at Waukegan, but not as many as used to. Afternoons, after work, and before Damyan got home from school, she'd walk down to the beach by the harbor. She'd listen to the halyards clack against the masts of the sailboats not yet taken ashore for winter. But she didn't come to look at the boats, small ones or big ones. She'd go down there to watch the waves, white as they crushed into shore, yellow as they withdrew. Plastic detergent bottles bobbed in with the current and bobbed out again.

Always, Maritsa would tell herself, the first betrayal, leaving, will always be the worst. She was confused by her own choices and her own desires, and she'd look out the windows of the houses she cleaned, at the enormous leafless trees, trees that took almost all the space of the sky, and curse herself for not knowing what to dream. Is this an answer? A husband panting into the phone? Days wandering rooms of other people's piles of things?

Damyan looked so unlike his father that people in their building used to whisper that someone else must have been parking in her garage. She'd been called a whore behind her back so many times that for years she'd felt like one. Honorary whore of a building that apparently needed one. Damyan was a pale, oval-headed boy, with little hair and large, fearlessly unblinking eyes. He wasn't afraid to look at anybody, and often adults were put in the uncomfortable position of having to turn away from a child's stare. He had all his father's curiosity and none of his mother's restlessness. *What's the difference between snot and saliva? Why do people say you can drink one and not the other? They're both only secretions. I've tried snot and it's possible, you can drink as much as you want.* His father's boy, already exasperating teachers on a new continent. He was also a courageous kid and knew he had to buck up for his mother in a country that wasn't so much unkind to her as ambivalent. His mother had always been a woman people talked about, and not only because she'd always been the prettiest. Now, here in Waukegan, she shamed him. He tried not to let her know. He kept silent. And some nights she'd sit on the floor of his room and rest her head against his mattress and ask, Is it Daddy? *No.* Is it home? *No.* Why won't you tell me? The boy would dig his face into his pillow and feign sleep.

The second betrayal was named Ted. He was from Pakistan. His name wasn't Ted any more than Damyan's was Danny. I'm Ted, he'd said, Ted tired of correcting people. She almost laughed. "That's not funny," she said. How long since she'd laughed? A ten-minute break during class, the two of them leaning against a set of little lockers. He'd looked at her then from an odd angle, his head too far to the left. He looked at her as if he already knew her weaknesses and was mocking her for bothering to try to hide them. He spoke English; he only pretended he didn't. "It's my second language," he said, "but don't tell anybody that we speak English in Pakistan, I'm here for dates. Night school ESL is the United Nations of Women. Filipinos, Mexicans, Koreans, Somalis, where did you say you were from again?" All this she laughed at, quietly, the way she remembered laughing as a child at things she knew she wasn't supposed to, pressing her fingers into her lips. She thought it wouldn't be right to ask his real name, that it would somehow break the grip he was already beginning to have on her. He would always be Ted, even after he was gone, and he had smooth lips that she knew would soon kiss her places Lyubomir couldn't have imagined.

Which is what happened, for three months, but mostly they watched television and ate bag after bag of sour cream and onion Doritos. They'd talk about how fat real Americans were compared to TV Americans, except for Roseanne and her husband. (Why aren't their kids fat, though?) They'd sit and wonder whether they'd bloom out like sandbags after they got their citizenship. Ted was a small man, half the size of Lyubomir. She could have picked him up and tossed him. They'd talk about how stupid the shows were, and how this stupidity, which was genuine stupidity, was something to laugh at, but also to be wary of. All the dollars in the universe, Ted would murmur, and this is what they do with it.

One night, after two in the morning, the two of them on the

living-room floor, naked beneath a thin blanket, the TV light casting a gray pallor over the furniture, the volume down so low all they could hear was faint laughter, and suddenly the child in the bedroom begins to shout. Amid all the unrecognizable words, it was possible to make out: *Dyado! Dyado!* Ted's first thought was that it meant father, that the crafty boy knew the only way to rid his mother's house of this interloper was to cry at the worst possible moment. After she'd buttoned her shirt and gone to the boy's room, he'd remained on the floor, motionless, a couch cushion beneath his head. Maritsa. She told him she'd been named after a river. He tries to picture a river quietly gurgling through a snow-hushed forest in a country that he will never see. Yet he's never had any talent for conjuring trees or woods or rivers, and the image gives way to her face.

Now she is back from the boy's room, settled under the throw, her head next to his on the cushion. She rubs his wrist.

"Hey."

"What was that about?"

"It's all right."

"His father?"

"No."

"No?"

"Only a nightmare."

Maritsa told him a strange thing then. She spoke in his ear. In the dream, Damyan had been shouting, not for Lyubomir, but for his grandfather, her father, a man who died before Damyan was even born. He was warning him about a truck. A famous family story. The kid must have heard it a thousand times.

"My father was hit by a truck, but he lived. The story is always told this way. After the war, Dyado got hit by a truck on

Ravoski Street. He was flattened—he never walked again—but he didn't die. The Slavs couldn't kill him, the Germans couldn't kill him, the Russians couldn't kill him. Not even a truck."

They lay in the silence, the TV light crawling, then retreating across the walls.

Later, years later, Ted will think of that night. A woman named Maritsa. The two of them on the floor. Her boy shouting in the night, warning a man already long dead. *Dyado, the truck!* Are warnings ever timely?

Damyan stares at his mother. They're at the post office mailing letters. Her mascara makes her eyes look too wide open.

"What is it?"

"Ted doesn't come anymore."

"No."

"Why not?"

She looks past the top of her son's head, through the slits in the blinds, at the pieces of cars flinging by. *You chased him away. Anyway, it wasn't love. I've ruined your father.* She says nothing.

The boy waits, looks at his mother, and knows she will keep taking walks, alone, even after his father comes, if his father comes, and that the walks will have nothing to do with her friend from English class, or any other man, including his father. Still, he tries to be kind.

"Maybe he'll come back," he says.

LATE DUSK, JOSLIN, ILLINOIS

Even the shadows are green tonight. Deb watches the moon. It's out early. Also, it is too hot for October and the crickets are confused. By October they are supposed to shriek less loudly. By October their hysteria is supposed to dissipate. By October there is supposed to be calm. By October — not this October, another one — she promised herself she'd be gone. She once said to Carl, If you were a real man, you'd get me the hell out of here. He just looked at her and scratched his cheek. He wasn't a man to answer when spoken to like that. Not taking the bait was his specialty. If Carl were a fish, he'd live forever. Either that or he'd starve. But even she has to admit there's beauty in this green, practically breathable light. The land stretching away into it. The power line towers also. Even the driveway. Even the shed. All coated. All still. Carl says the land is here for us to build on. Here for us to expand on. That's what it's here for. As soon as the fiscal year is through, he's going make an appointment to talk to the architect. The permits will have been approved by then and so —

Weather said a storm this afternoon but it never came. She likes to watch the storms meander this way from out beyond

Dixon. The lightning like a jabbing finger choosing, choosing. Now the light itself is enough. Carl's on his way home, singing along to the radio unless there's a commercial. Sometimes he even sings to those. Carl, you stupid fuck. The land will bury you. This land, any land. Least any sane person would do is leave. How many times do I have to say it? Deb gulps the light, wishing she hated it, wishing she didn't only want to stand here and watch it tonight, wishing for courage, stupidity, anything other than curiosity. This strange, breathable light, this life-blood light.

PART IV

Country of Us

*After a while he spoke to the floor.
"It's over me like a ton of water, the
things I don't know."*

— GINA BERRIAULT, "AROUND
THE NEAR RUIN"

WALDHEIM

Louie was a bookbinder and died poor, and so a burial society called the Sons of Maccabee dug him a grave at Waldheim, a fallow field west of Chicago on the banks of the Des Plaines River. For years he'd been paying that outfit seven dollars annually for a two-plot. As long as he paid up, he figured, he wouldn't croak. This notion proved true until March 1941. But here's the thing: when the time came near for his wife, Rachel, thirty-plus years later, she flat out refused to go to Waldheim. It wasn't that she hadn't loved him. She had. His dumbo ears, his monologues from the toilet. The way he never sat in a chair without taking his belt off first. But she said now that her daughter's husband had money, they'd have to kill her first before she stuck one dead toenail way the hell out there at Waldheim. They buried her in Skokie near the new mall in the early seventies. Of course, Louie doesn't know this, and by his calculations Rachel must be getting on near a hundred and thirty, and he continues to marvel at the strength of her constitution and the progress of modern medicine while at the same time chastising himself for being lonely and wishing that it would end so that she would come to him.

ON THE 14

On the Mission bus today I sat across from Uncle Horace who has been dead for twenty-odd years. The last time I saw him was at Aunt Molly's in Fall River. On the bus, he looked tired. He was barefoot. He looked like he didn't want to talk. When I knew him, Uncle Horace always wanted to talk. He always wanted to tell you who he knew. Horace was a man who made great claims of knowing people. Chiang Kai-shek, Julius Rosenwald, Oliver Wendell Holmes. Shake the hand that shook the hand that shook the hand of John L. Sullivan! On the bus, he was bedraggled, as if God had left him out in the rain for decades. The bus was hot and crowded, our breath was clouding the windows. There was no room to take off our coats. At Fourteenth and Mission, an enormous teetering woman with uncountable numbers of Safeway bags got on and my uncle shot up from his seat, swooped his arm, and announced, *Madam, to your rest!*

Standing, my uncle was hunchbacked. He'd always had great posture. ("At Eton," he used to say, "we always ate sitting to the trot.") On the bus he was so stooped over I could have set a table on him, and would have, too, if I'd had some dishes. We could have had tea and crumpets like old times. Bent, drenched, broke, pilloried, my dead uncle. He slipped the woman with the bags of groceries his card and told her to come by his office Tuesday after lunch.

"I'm back from the club by 2:30 at the latest. Bring your checkbook, My Lady. Or cash."

He began moving through the crowd, handing out his card. "Wise up, people. Money begets money. You want to ride the 14 for the rest of your lives?"

When my stop was next, I yanked the cord and got up, stood by the middle door. A moment later, a moist, oddly soft hand enwrapped my neck. I turned to him, and he spoke as if I was me but also as if this didn't matter, as if my being myself, whoever this was, couldn't have less to do with anything.

"Nobody can take them away from you," he said, his little face bunched, his shoulders rising past his ears.

"What?"

Those fingers on my neck, not holding exactly, only resting, almost as though he were gently feeling my pulse, as if I was the one —

"The lies you tell are the only things that stay," Horace said. "Truth won't get you a cup of coffee in hell. Forget about the Ritz, honey."

"But," I said, "because of your lies, they all died broke. Wilbert, Flo, Nelson, Dotty, Shirley, Ida, Molly — Grandma Sarah used to say that you went for everybody in town's quarters, but when it came to relations, you went for their nickels, too."

"A tony relative in every family. You play your part, you do your share."

"And everyone ponied up — except Irv Pincus, who could always smell a rat when a rat — "

"Still, not a bad record."

"Yes, and it was you—"

"It was I!"

"Proud?"

"I was loaded. They all wanted what I had. I'm to blame? I'm criminal?"

"But the only reason you had what you had was because they gave you all their money."

"A technicality!"

"Grandpa Walt dropped dead after reading his bank statement."

"Your grandfather had a weak heart. Not to mention no stomach for business."

"Your own son—Monroe—finally went bonkers. They had to lock him up at Taunton State five years ago."

"The Ginsburgs have no lunacy."

"He literally tore his hair out of his head with his hands—"

"Must have been his mother's side."

"Remorse?"

Uncle Horace stood up a little straighter. "A legacy, boy, a legacy. May you leave one yourself. That way you wouldn't have to steal mine. Then again, how much do you think it's worth? How about we go 70/30? Go ahead sell it, sell it all!"

"And Josephine?"

"Leave her out of this happy reunion."

"I mean the humiliation—"

"I said leave her out—"

"—to beg for handouts from her own flesh and blood, the very people you plundered—"

"Not once did she beg. Listen: Nobody didn't love Josephine. If I'd been the Boston Strangler, they'd have given us all—"

"And they did! They did!"

"And may you for a single day of your life, for one hour, know the kind of love that I—"

The doors flapped open: Twentieth Street. Before he stepped down, Uncle Horace leaned to me. That old smell again, of Aunt Molly's. A reek of bleach and onions. He smooched one ear, then the other.

"Sayonara, turkeyboy."

LONGFELLOW

My brother used to terrorize me with a small rubber hippopotamus named Longfellow. He was about the size of a tooth, and he spoke in an extremely high, piercing voice. Longfellow said it wasn't my fault I was so limited intellectually, that it was simply the luck of the draw and with hard work, and perhaps some family connections, one day I might be able to eke out a living. Now, Big Bill Thompson-Fox was the mayor of the town where Longfellow lived. Unlike Longfellow, the mayor was kind to me. The town was called Pubic, Illinois. Big Bill Thompson-Fox was a finger puppet of a fox in a policeman's uniform and my brother endowed him with the gentle, patient drawl of Sheriff Andy Taylor. A child psychologist might say that Longfellow and Big Bill Thompson-Fox represented the two sides of my brother's nature. On the one hand, I was his brother and he hated me, and on the other hand, I was his brother and he loved me. I don't know. All I know is that Big Bill's kindness barely made a dent, because even though he had a relatively important job (part-time mayor of a town of about 550 Pubians) and Longfellow didn't seem to have a job at all, the mayor was no match for the hippo.

I also lived in Pubic, or my voice did. I was the voice of the Matchbox Chevrolet Caprice that served as Big Bill Thompson-Fox's limousine. I wasn't supposed to say any words. The car didn't know any. My role was to make automotive noises at appropriate moments. As I say, Longfellow's chief preoccupation was making me cry, but he also spent much of his time and energy disrupting city council meetings and haranguing Big Bill Thompson-Fox for things like misappropriation of public funds, giving out no-bid contracts to shadowy underworld cronies, and in general fostering a culture of corruption that pervaded Pubic from the lowliest branch post office to the fifth floor of City Hall. One day Longfellow advocated impeachment of Big Bill after he allowed me (i.e., his car) to vote on an important resolution that would have limited fluorocarbon emissions. Longfellow claimed that it was a blatant conflict of interest. For the record, I voted against the resolution, because I felt that any restrictions on the auto industry would have resulted in the loss of American jobs. After Longfellow raised his loud objections (*Kickbacks! Backroom dealing! Sweetheart deals!*), Big Bill Thompson-Fox, in what I thought was a pretty brilliant switcheroo, claimed that my vote actually hadn't counted, that it was nonbinding. "In certain circumstances," Mayor Thompson-Fox said, "interested members of the public may, according to our charter, weigh in, in a purely advisory capacity, on matters of particular interest, in order to give them more of a voice in government. It's a unique and quite participatory feature of our democracy here in Pubic. It's actually based on a pre-Napoleonic French model."

"Ah ha, Chevrolet. I knew all along there was something francophone about that car!"

"Please, sir, we'll have no unseemly outbursts."

"Oh, you and your *Robert's Rules of Order...*"

"Bailiff!" Big Bill Thompson-Fox cried. "Where's the bailiff?"

I made car noises to the effect that we didn't have a bailiff on the payroll.

Longfellow would not be silenced. Big Bill Thompson-Fox and his car remained on the carpet. It was Longfellow who attained the heights of the prophet. My brother set the hippo on his head and intoned: "Taxidermy without representation is tyranny. If this be treason, you can kiss my ass back to the Zambezi."

In 1990, I found Longfellow in a drawer in my mother's house, along with some rolling papers (my mother's), circa 1975. He'd survived my parents' divorce, three moves, and two remarriages, the little shit. I held a summary trial. Longfellow stood accused of assault, slander, noise pollution, and a myriad of immigration violations.

"Any last words?"

"Yo, toothache, what's with the shilly-shally? If you're going to do it, do it."

I popped his head off with a toenail clipper. And though there was ample evidence (the clipper in my hand, the severed head on the carpet, a tattered but unused bus ticket to Joliet), I could not be prosecuted, because the municipality where the execution allegedly occurred no longer existed and local criminal statutes could not apply. Under the letter of the law, you can't be found guilty of killing anybody in Atlantis unless you can dredge up that jurisdiction from the bottom of the sea. Same is true for Narnia, Bedrock, and Nimh, where the brave rats live. Nonetheless, technicalities aside, there is the human heart to consider. The only certain thing is, you'll be brothers forever, my mother used to say. Everything else in your entire life — health, money, sex — is all a crapshoot.

I clip his head off and still — still, thy brother's blood cries out in a high high voice only dogs and myself can hear.

PADDY BAULER IN A QUIET MOMENT

DeLuxe Gardens, 403 West North Avenue, 1964

The clown prince had them. All his raucous talk, his famous quotable lines, and yet there were certain nights, late in his career, when, if there was no committee meeting or funeral or wake or wedding, the once-mighty alderman would shoo out the stragglers and lock the door. This particular boozing shed is closed. And the man himself would slump on a stool, quiet, and face himself in the mirror of his own bar. *Mr. Bauler, sir, aren't you on the wrong side of the slab?* Think about it. A real conundrum. When you're Paddy Bauler, you can't go and see Paddy Bauler. And he laughs. Not out loud, an inside laugh, the kind you can carry around for hours, days, years even, the kind of laugh you might carry to the end if you don't take yourself too seriously. But here's another conundrum. Lately he's stopped laughing all that much, outside or inside laughs. A German, he's been playing an Irishman so long he's started to dream of his own boggy grave. Used to be that it was all laughs—and votes. Now, that's how you run a city. A vote is loyalty and loyalty is a vote…a lifetime of them. See? Easy. From the cradle to the grave. (Casket courtesy of the Democratic Party.) And you're either constant to the party or you aren't constant to the party. No such thing as halfway. Independent? Ha! Go see Paddy Bauler. Heal me, Ward Heeler.

A mammoth man, but soft all over. A. J. Liebling described him as more gravel pit than mountain. He used to wrestle himself on the floor of the mayor's office for the personal entertainment of His Honor Mayor Anton Cermak himself.

Cermak martyred, the lucky Bohemian. Pat Nash gone. Ed Kelly gone. *Paddy Bauler? Is that antediluvian still kicking around?*

Hey, Paddy, spot me a drink. You know I'm good for it. Don't I always carry my precinct for you?

Paddy, my boiler's busted. They want three hundred and fifty bucks.

Hey, Paddy, listen, Paddy. My son. Knocked his old lady around a little. Talk to Sergeant Itagopian for me?

Paddy, it's my mother — the cancer —

Paddy, it's Eddie Gabinik; don't you remember me?

Paddy?

Paddy?

Mr. Bauler? Sir?

GERALDO, 1986

He warns us that what's inside might not be appropriate for children and other sensitive viewers. Al Capone's lost vault. They're tearing down the Lexington Hotel, once the Big Tuna's headquarters, and have discovered a vault that's been sealed for decades. Who knew he lost one? Who even cared? But now that Chicago knows it, the city is awash in hysterical anticipation. And Geraldo's got the exclusive. *Live.* I'm alone in front of the TV with a joint and a hunk of cheese. There's a team of hard-hatted workmen with jackhammers and high explosives. There are wafts of dust and lots of noise, and Geraldo whisper-shouts into the microphone. *We're making history here.* It goes on for more than an hour and a half, with frequent commercial breaks.

At one point Geraldo says, "I feel like Jeremiah walking among the ruins."

Look, Geraldo, just open the damn thing already.

Finally, they blast the door off. Geraldo coughs, gasps, says something inaudible — there's an enormous crash. The camera jumbles and the screen goes blank. Cut to another commercial. Geraldo's dead and they're selling antacid. And Oldsmobiles and Mountain Dew. And then he's back, undaunted. Geraldo Rivera knows no daunted. Wait. He's holding something. A bottle. Ladies and gentlemen, citizens of Chicago, interested parties around the world, we've made a discovery. Pause. Swallow. Alphonsus Capone—alias Scarface alias Big Tuna alias Jolly Fellow alias Snorky—may have once drunk from this very bottle before carrying out yet another despicable act, the likes of which have made this city infamous around the globe. Go to the deepest Amazon, as I have, Geraldo says, and there you might meet, as I did, a little native boy, naked, nothing but a loincloth hardly covering his burgeoning private parts, and tell him, as I did, that you are from Chicago, and he'll say, Chicago! Chicago! Capone! Pow! Pow! Kill! Kill! Kill! Yes, the lips of such a man may have once touched the phallic spout of this very bottle...

The camera zooms in on the bottle's label. *Ernest and Julio Gallo, 1981.* Pans back to Geraldo's stricken face. Maybe someone back at the station was thinking, Now at last we'll get rid of this moron. Geraldo looks as if he wants to eat the microphone's afro. Not much can leave this man wordless. But I keep watching, we all keep watching. The wonder of live television—even after nothing's happened, it keeps happening. Plus, there is always the chance that Geraldo might spontaneously combust. Soldier on, Geraldo, we're still with you.

"Friends," his voice rising to a squeal. "Friends, how on earth did this bottle, this vessel of Dionysus, find its way through the impregnable walls of a sealed vault? Only in a city as diseased as this one, where vice still flows like milk down an innocent child's throat, like blood in the veins, like sewage in the sanitation canal, could one of the greatest robbers in the history of the known world be himself robbed, the thief thieved, the boodler boodled. Oh, my friends, mystery begets mystery begets mystery — it's the very fornication of existence in this modern Gomorrah we call Chicago.

What were we expecting? That the vault would be our King Tut's tomb? Pompeii in the Loop? Maybe we were just heartened that, even here, something could survive, something remain. In a city where all is knocked down and all is replaced, maybe we just want to know something has been here all along. A solitary man holds a bottle and a microphone amid plumes of old dust. Nobody gives a damn what's in the vault, Geraldo. Times like these all you want is to hear a voice, any voice. In the afternoons, I bag groceries at the Dominicks on Skokie Highway. I'm seventeen. When I get fired, which will be soon, the manager will say, Listen, putz, you'll never work at a Dominicks again, anywhere in the Chicagoland area and northern Indiana — you got it, You're not competent, you lack basic competences. Mostly though, I'm just lonely, a new kind of lonely. I'd think about all the eyes that would never look my way, all the eyes that were always turning away. Do you remember? When all you had was your own sweaty needs, your own endless furious needs?

HAROLD WASHINGTON WALKS AT MIDNIGHT

Out at Midway Airport

No one in this city, no matter where they live or how they live, is free from the fairness of my administration. We'll find you and be fair to you wherever you are.

— HAROLD WASHINGTON, 51ST MAYOR OF CHICAGO

Of Harold Washington, people used to say that as long as he had a political fight on his hands he'd never be lonely, and that was all well and good while he was alive, but it caused problems for the mayor in heaven. After a few years of paying his dues as an aldermanic-level angel, he challenged Gabriel for archangel and nearly pulled it off with 47.6 percent of the vote. Disgruntled and jealous cherubs supported him in droves. Finally, God's chief of staff, just to get rid of him for a while, let Harold Washington come home for a small, unannounced visit.

It was Martha who spotted him by the baggage claim, long after the last flight had come and gone. She was sweeping up, the last hour of her shift. She said his face had the haggard look of someone who has been crying for years, one way or another.

"Do you know what I mean?" she asked her friend Lucy, the only person she told this to, the only person who would believe her. The two of them were having lunch in the employee cafeteria. Lucy said she knew what she meant. She understood that a man's dry face could have the look of weeping. She mentioned her uncle Jomo. "He had the look, too. Uncle Jomo's wife died while he was still in his thirties. He put his grief on with his clothes every morning. When did you see the mayor?"

"Last Thursday," Martha said.

"Did he say anything?"

"Not at first. I went up and told him that the Orlando flight came in an hour ago. There's no more bags, sir. You can contact the luggage office in the morning. Everybody from Delta's gone home. Then he turned to me with a finger on his lips and I knew."

"How'd he look?" Lucy asked.

"Thinner."

"No! When that man was done eating chicken, he'd start in on the table legs."

"All of it gone. And his shoulders were stooped—bony, really," Martha said. "His trench coat looked like it was hanging off two doorknobs."

Lucy watched her friend. She had that good way of listening—with her elbows on the table and her hands propping up her face like two bookends. Neither of them was eating anymore.

"Our burdens," Lucy said.

"Yes," Martha said.

"My God, remember," Lucy said. "They wouldn't let the man do a thing. The mayor would want to take a leak and Eddy Vrdolyak would vote against it."

"I remember, I remember," Martha said. "How could anybody not remember?"

"You forget how people forget."

"Mmmmm."

"What about his eyes?"

"Still beautiful."

"So what'd he say?"

"He said Midway looks like a real airport now. Richie Daley, I said, and he looked at me with those eyes. I said, I hate to break it to you, Mr. Mayor, but Richie is king now, and he shouted, Richie Daley, that unworthy dauphin? The father was one thing, a monster but a man with innate political talent, even brains, a man who somehow — somehow — kept his own nostrils clean while the putrescence of corruption oozed around him. No, the father was one thing. But if Richie Daley is the second coming, I'm Annette Funicello."

Martha gasping, laughing. "The Mouseketeer?"

"That's what he said. Even made those ears behind his head with his fingers."

"And he laughed? He laughed?"

"Half-laughed, half didn't."

"I know what you mean."

"Then he cleared his throat, all *mayoral*, and asked if the pay was any better now that this is a real airport. I said, 'Sir, there haven't been any other miracles besides you.' And then he did laugh, Luce. He laughed until what was left of his poor body wasn't there anymore."

RENTERS

Frank had never been one to fight back in the heat of any moment. He would usually wait a few days and then state his opposition to some plan or another of hers without warning. As a strategy for getting his way this usually failed miserably. Marie had just stepped out of the tub when he announced: "Since when have you needed my permission for anything, ever?"

"Is this an ambush?"

He tried to hand her a towel, but she wouldn't take it.

"You're wet."

"Am I?" Marie said. "Really?"

"I've been giving it thought."

"It?"

"The firearm we discussed."

"Oh, that. I'm not asking. I want it. They're two entirely different things."

"We're going to keep up with the treatments. Another six months and we'll know—"

"Bad enough every doctor lies to me, but to have you, too. I know it, I feel it. Frankly, Frank—"

"Please, no frankly Franks —"

"Don't make me laugh. Hurts."

"— and if we want a second opinion before then, we can always go to Sioux Falls —"

"Whether I'd ever have the guts is another story. I want the comfort. That's all. Look at me."

"I'm looking."

"Fuck Sioux Falls."

He tried giving her the towel again. She wouldn't take it and stood there, water still on her bony shoulders.

"Now you're looking."

"Not very comfortable for me."

"You? We're talking about you?"

A half hour later, he went down into the basement and rummaged around. Most of their stuff was still unpacked from the move. He found his 20-gauge in a narrow cardboard box that also held the vacuum cleaner and a barbell. A few times a year he went pheasant hunting with colleagues from his department. He walked slowly up the stairs. She was standing at the kitchen sink with a mug of coffee. He put the shotgun on the table.

"That?"

"I'll have to buy some shells."

"Something for under my pillow, Frank. You know I'm talking about something for under my pillow."

A few weeks later, Frank drove by the old house. Was it a few weeks? Lack of sleep was warping time. It was six-thirty in the evening in mid-September and the glass in the big front window was burning in the slowly dissipating light. Frank slowed down, considered stopping, but didn't. It felt disloyal to even look at the place. Still, the farther away from the house he drove, the more he saw the blur of those flames in the window.

Cleaned out, not much of a trace of the years they spent there except possibly the remains of Marie's garden. Years ago, Frank had built a snow fence to protect the garden from the wind. Marie would spend Sunday hours out there, squatting and puttering, talking to her plants, coaxing the soil. He thinks of a few stubborn tomatoes, withered lettuce, some hearty beets. Between the two tall maples in the side yard, there might be a few broken plastic clothespins in the dirt. Moving your stuff out of a place is like unloading a ship, except an empty house doesn't sail away beyond the horizon. It sits there and waits for you to return. All you have to do one day is head west, on Route 14, because you don't want to go home right away, and there it is, halfway to Volga, the house, their house. It was never theirs, legally, anyway. Though they didn't have to be, Marie and Frank were renters, they'd always be renters. They'd never wanted to be beholden. Renting had always felt more free. They could always pick up and move somewhere else, which must be why they never did. If you execute the choice, you lose the choice. When they finally did move back to Brookings to be closer to the clinic, they thought about buying a place, but they were in their mid-fifties now. What would be the point? Especially now. All things being equal, which they weren't, wouldn't rent and a mortgage amount to pretty much the same thing for a couple without kids? In their mid-forties, they'd said the same thing. How did they think they'd avoid becoming beholden? Frank turned the car around. As he drove back east, he passed the house once again and thought of them at the windows. How many times had the two of them stood at those windows?

Neither Marie nor Frank was a native. In 1975, they'd moved here from Chicago to teach at South Dakota State. Marie was a Nineteenth-Century Americanist; Frank taught classics. While the favorite pastime of many of their colleagues was to try and conjure up what heinous crime they must have committed in some other life to deserve exile in this moonscape among the earnest corn-fed, Marie and Frank had come, over the years, to consider eastern South Dakota the only place that would ever be home. Surrounded on all sides by the gentle undulations out near the edge of the horizon. To call this flat isn't really to look at it. The land rolls, as if it's always in motion. The switch grass leaning away from the wind. Here and there a clump of trees, and a little over a mile from home, or what used to be home, but still on the property, a hidden arroyo, a private wound in the earth. Only Marie and Frank knew where it was.

But for those front windows, the house itself had been nothing special. The bedrooms were tiny squares, though there were more of them than they needed. They each had one of their own for an office, and one together, which made them feel a little ludicrous and also rich. Sometimes they'd invite each other to their office. Even as recently as a couple of years ago, they still did things like that, slide messages under the doors of their own house. *Hey. You busy?* Once or twice a summer, they chained Rudy up (they hated to do it, Rudy liked nothing more than roaming when they took walks, this was the single exception), walked to the arroyo, climbed down to that grove of soft sand, and put down a blanket. Nobody knew it. It wasn't like they showed off to their friends. Look at us, after all these years. Marie's long red hair spread across the blanket. Rudy howling—

She'd stopped appearing in his dreams. Now he's afraid to fall asleep. Lying there beside her, awake, hours, awake—most disloyal of all, he's begun to remember her.

It was Marie who had found the house. It was Marie who had insisted, so many years ago now, that they move outside of Brookings. Frank had protested, asked what would be the point, it's not like we're tenant farmers. But Marie said, If we're going to live here, let's at least endure the landscape.

"You mean experience?"

"That, too."

It had been a long time since anybody farmed the land that went with the house. Schactler, their old landlord, had two other farms in Beadle County but always meant to restart operations on theirs. Every time he came by to collect the rent, he said, "Won't be long now before you hear the sound of the tractor out here, you two won't mind a little noise?" But neither of his sons came home from college in the East as they'd promised. Nothing made Schactler prouder than that his sons were too good to come home to South Dakota and work the land with their father. Even so, he slaved away, keeping the other farms going, and so was content to get a little house rent off the third place. Schactler once said renting a house was one thing, to rent out land another. He couldn't stomach what another man might do with it. Like your woman, he said, winking at Frank. Marie said Schactler might be an unreconstructed Neanderthal, but what he said about land made sense. There's a way to call something sacred without getting high and mighty about it. After his wife died, Schactler slowly began to slow down. He stopped talking farming the third farm, stopped talking about his boys coming home. Mrs. Schactler had been a kind, shrewd woman who always complimented Frank on Marie. *What's a homely-looking character doing with a fiery sass like that?* And she never got on them, even with her eyes, as God knows so many other people did for years, about: where were the children.

For years, in early May, Schactler used to light a controlled burn to prepare the fields around the house for the planting he never got around to doing. The glow of those fires. How they'd turn off all the lamps and stand at the window and watch the flames poke up into the night. Last he heard, Schactler was in a nursing home in Aberdeen. Soon his boys would come home to sell all three farms.

He thought of the way the night wind would press against the big window, as if someone were out in the dark pushing against it with both hands.

In the old kitchen, her head lying on a stack of student papers, her eyes wide open, the sun a rising layer of pink on the outer fields.

"Come to bed."

"Tomorrow's tiring."

"Don't say that."

"Even the plants exhaust me, the toaster—"

Raising her head in the blue dawn, eyes blazing, not tired at all.

"Stop being terrified, Frank. We can't both be. Who'll remember to feed the dog?"

"Isn't arroyo a gorgeous word?" Marie asked.

"It is."

"Origin?"

"Everyone else around here says creek, it's only us—"

"Origin?"

"Spanish. Pre-Roman."

"It's like a nook, a cranny. All my life I've been looking for a good cranny. Bury me here."

"Stop."

"It's just biology. It's all just biology."

"Marie."

"You won't?"

"Furthermore," Frank said, "it's a zoning issue. You can't just bury people—"

That night, after driving by the old house, he did find Rudy barking along the fence line of the new house when he pulled up. He leaped out of the car and flung open the front door and found Marie lying on the couch, her head thrown back against the armrest, a book on the floor. He ran across the carpet, knelt, and gripped her knees. He looked up at the bare walls. Their paintings and posters and framed photographs were still in boxes from the move, though they had already lived eight months in this new place. Couldn't he at least have unpacked a few and nailed up some pictures? Why had he waited so long?

He gripped her knees. The leash of the oxygen tank gently resting on her bare clavicle. After a moment, under his own heavy breathing, hers, shallow, nearly silent. He lifted his head and watched her sleep and waited for the relief that was sure to wash over him. He waited, and still it didn't come. *The fires, M., do you remember Schactler's fires?* Don't forgive me —

THE GATE

None but the wind should warn of your returning.

— TOWNES VAN ZANDT, "NONE BUT THE RAIN"

It wasn't visiting hours. They let me in anyway, after I begged from a wall phone on the first floor. She was on the third floor. I needed a special code to work the elevator. After I buzzed, I was led into the TV room, which was also a lunchroom. She was waiting there, holding a book. I can't remember what the title was, but I remember staring at the cover. It had a drawing of an ornate iron gate. Beyond the gate was a gray sea. We sat across from each other. She laughed. She told me about a guy who earlier that morning had called his mother from the phone at the nurses' station and shouted, so the entire floor could hear, could she please get him out of here so he could kill himself in peace. She pointed to a boy — he couldn't have been more than sixteen or seventeen — sitting at one of the lunch tables listening to headphones, peacefully drumming the table with his palms. That's him, she said. He'll be all right.

"You'll be all right, too," I said.

"It doesn't really matter."

"You will."

"Don't say it again, all right?"

I looked around the room. In the corner was a pile of tattered boxes of board games. A stack of old magazines. There was a computer inside what looked like a video arcade game, the screen behind thick glass, a keyboard dangling from a chain.

"I brought you a brownie," I said.

We used to say we lived in the country of us. I've never been able to explain this to anyone, though everyone I have told has nodded like they understood. Nine years we lived there. I watched her eat a brownie.

"Aren't I thin?"

"You're too thin."

"Want some brownie?"

"No, I brought it for you."

"Take some."

She handed me a piece of the brownie. Our fingers met. A half hour later, the kind small man with an accent—Polish?—unlocked the door and let me out.

A couple of years before I was born, my mother took my four-year-old brother and ran away from my father, home to Massachusetts and her parents, where they holed up like fugitives. She said she wouldn't go back to Chicago if she was dragged by a train. My brother had a field day with Grandpa Walt, staying up all night eating doughnuts and talking about whether Johnson would dump Humphrey from the ticket. A week later, my father flew east. He knelt on the sidewalk with white roses and sang her name. Neighbors watched the drama from behind their curtains. Phones rang up and down Robeson Street. Mavis, can you get more romantic with a capital R? But those days before he showed up, I think about them, the stillness of my mother's mornings. Something peaceful about the possibility of my own nonexistence. My mother didn't go see any of her friends. The farthest she ventured from her old bedroom was the backyard, where she sat on the huge boulder she used to sit on as a kid, her chin in her hand, and Grandpa Walt would call out the window of his study, Hey, would you look at the thinker perched on her rock? except that now he didn't say anything, only watched her, she being twenty-six and married now.

FALL RIVER, 1967

My mother stands by the window, holding a duster, listening to Frank Zappa. Like a lot of people, she pretended to like the music more than she actually did, which is what Zappa himself counted on. He figured if people pretended long enough, they might actually start to listen. No one's here but me, and I am three and a half and asleep. She dusts a little, but there's something about the song, the stopping and the starting, the half-talking, half-singing—Movin' to Montana soon, Gonna be a Dental Floss tycoon—that makes her want to refuse in principle to do anything productive. Zappa's pretty out there, her friend Judy had said when she gave her the record. It isn't a place my mother is at all against going—out there. Now I am awake and shrieking. To buy a minute or two, she turns up the volume. My mother examines the duster. It is made of some sort of feathers and she wonders what dead bird was worth this clean apartment, or anybody's.

CHICAGO, 1974

*I*t may have been in The Wapshot Chronicle *where someone — the grandmother? — leaves* Middlemarch *outside during a storm. All those heroically screwed-up lives — all those hopes, all those beautiful failures — bloated with rain. It made me think of my mother in her room. Sometimes she'd stay up all night, reading.* Middlemarch *was always on the table beside the bed. It was the guest room, but we called it her room. She no longer shared my father's. We didn't have many guests. The door's locked. Sometimes at night my father comes and tries the knob.*

HIGHLAND PARK, 1978

THE MOORS OF CHICAGO

We'd go out to the hill at night, Stu Barkus and me, and sometimes the moon was out and we could see each other's lips move in the dark. Old conversations dry up like rain. I haven't seen Barkus in years. I tried calling him after I heard his father died, but the number I had didn't work.

Still, out there, there was an easiness, the rare kind of easiness you get with someone you've known so long there's no need to prove anything. Sometimes we'd smoke a little, talk some more, but now that I'm thinking of the hill, mostly what I remember is us not talking. And I remember remembering. My parents used to take my brother and me up to the hill. My mother would lie on her back and stare at the sky. My father would talk. My mother would look at the sky and sometimes answer him, sometimes not. I'd run around in circles in the grass. From the very top you could see the lake. My mother called the hill the moors of Chicago. It wasn't until I read but didn't finish *Wuthering Heights* in college that I understood what she was talking about, but even then I think I realized that there was something unhappy about the place. Maybe not the place itself exactly, but our place in it. It was too vast, too open, and too full of other people's laughter. Maybe this is why my parents brought us out there. Maybe they thought something would rub off on us. One time my father brought a kite he'd built from a kit. It was made of thin wooden sticks and paper so fine you could blow your nose with it. He spent an hour in the basement that morning gluing the kite together. He got it off the ground, but the wind ripped the spindle — is it called a spindle? — out of my hand, and the kite fluttered and took a nosedive into the grass. I cheered. Then I went over and jumped on it, crushed it to pieces.

Out there with Stu Barkus under the moon, I remembered this and told him about it. He listened. Barkus didn't tell his own stories. He didn't tell me, for instance, as I might have done, about a time he betrayed his own father's small attempt at something approximating love. If he said anything at all, I don't remember what it was. He may only have nodded his head in the dark.

My father tried, my mother tried. They knew they'd end sooner or later. In the meantime, we had to live. So they took us out to the moors, a mythical place that we all thought existed. Other people's laughter on the wind. My mother on the grass staring at the sky, my father talking, my brother reading. I was the youngest, wandering in circles.

BELIEF, 1999

An old Communist who believed in it once and for all time, but who also, almost from the very beginning, nursed a healthy animosity for the liars who carried it out and fouled it up — so he was never considered by anyone who mattered to be a very good Communist — walks the streets of Nusle in northwest Prague with hunched shoulders. Feet no good anymore, and so he shuffles, wanders, watches the changes, watches the young men and their cars, watches the apartment balconies crumble. What good was believing? And yet the alternative was not having faith in his fellow men, and isn't this another way of dying? Now he shuffles and watches, not hating any of it, any of them, but at the same time lording over them like the god he always swore he never wanted to be, and yet, if there's been any change at all in him after thirty-two years of heavy labor at Poldi Kladno, it is this: that he's so old now he *is* like a god, not participating, only watching, not giving any opinions, not scoffing, not pointing his glass and spouting off in the pub about the way things were then — none of that. Only existing, whatever this means, if it can mean anything for a man who no longer has the strength to work.

And even the love he once had for Marketa has boiled down and hardened, so that it's not even a memory anymore. More like one of the rocks she used to line up on the windowsill in the kitchen. He can pick it up and hold it, but it doesn't jolt him. Marketa used to tell him not to be so serious, that he was always so serious, watching himself as though from a camera on the wall. You a movie star, Bohumil?

*I*rv Pincus used to steal lamps from Kaplan's Furniture and turn around and sell them in the alley at a deep discount. As a salesman inside the store, the man was a lousy foot dragger, but in the alley Irv could really move the merchandise. The store's gone. In '66 the state of Massachusetts built I-195 smack through downtown. Kaplan's gone. City Hall gone. Dug a hole right through Main Street. Eminent domain, the sovereign power to take property for necessary public good. What good the new highway ever did for this city other than allow the rest of the world to drive right by and ignore it, Walt never knew. But maybe this was the point. Don't slow down, people, otherwise you might notice what's been lost. When they tore his store down, Walt stood on the sidewalk and wept into his sleeve. Not the store itself he mourned but the hours he spent at his office window watching, among other things, Irv Pincus fleece him in broad daylight. Try explaining this to my wife. It's the pictures in my head, Sarah, it's the pictures in my head they're wrecking. How am I supposed to hold it all without the brick and mortar around to remind me? Walt Kaplan died a decade later at fifty-nine years old. But can't you see Irv Pincus out there behind the store, auctioning off $150 Hudson Bay lamps to the highest bidder? Shirtsleeves, his flabby arms swinging:

Do I hear a hundred? Ninety? Eighty-five? Fifty? Anybody? Forty, it's a deal. *The man outlived Walt Kaplan by more years than anybody in the family bothered to count. Irv relocated to Miami Beach and called it America, sand between his toes, bless his pilfering soul.*

FALL RIVER, MASSACHUSETTS, 1966

SHHHHHH, ARTHUR'S STUDYING

ROMAN UPHEAVEL TOPIC
OF A BOOK BY DR. KAPLAN
Can Cataline be cleared? The reputation of the Roman con-
spirator assigned to infamy in the polemics of Cicero has been
reclaimed...

— FALL RIVER HERALD NEWS, SEPTEMBER 25, 1968

Walt's brother Arthur was a quiet boy who grew into an accomplished man. When they were boys, it was always *Shhhhhh, Arthur's studying.* There's got to be at least one yeshiva *bucher* in every family and a yeshiva *bucher*'s got to have quiet. Go play outside, Walt, your brother's studying. And so Walt went to work in their father's furniture store and Arthur went to college, first to Brown and then to Columbia for his Ph.D. in classics. Arthur's face was pale. He always looked as though he'd been dusted with flour. This added to his gravitas, and Walt, like the rest of the family, was proud that Arthur looked the part of a scholar ghost.

Arthur's first and only book appeared in 1968. For a man who lived such a quiet life (he'd married a wan, squirrelly-looking girl and they lived in Brooklyn without children), the book turned out to be a bit scandalous. The title was innocuous enough: *Cataline and His Role in the Roman Revolution.* Yet the book was a surprisingly spirited, and graphic, defense of Cataline, a man who apparently made a lot of trouble two thousand years ago. Here he was now, wreaking havoc once again via the pen of meek little Arthur Kaplan, a man who came out of the womb speaking Latin. "They called him a villainous fiend, murderer, corrupter of youth and donkeys, venial proprietor, traitor, drunken debauchee, temple robber…Plutarch himself topped it off with the accusation that Cataline deflowered his own daughter."

And all this in the prologue.

What? the family gasped. What? Don't get us wrong. An author is an author is an author, and our Arthur is an author. His name's right there on the cover. But incest? Donkeys? Maybe he should have been out in the street playing stickball with Walt.

"Maybe nobody will read it."

"Ah yes. Of course, that's the ticket. Nobody will read it!"

"But we'll put it on the shelf."

"Yes, absolutely. We'll put it on the shelf."

Upon Arthur's triumphant return to Fall River, he gave a short speech at his alma mater, BMC Durfee High School, noting that the destruction of Cataline's reputation was the result of the same sort of mudslinging that characterizes the politics of today. "And if you think the Romans were violent? Maybe we ought to look at ourselves in this year, 1968. It is often not the great man who is ultimately heard but his detractors. Detractors always shout louder and use more colorful language. Elections bring out the poet in politicians, don't they? Take, for instance, the consular elections of 64 . ., when Cicero called Piso (father of Caesar's last wife, Calpurnia), among other things, brute, plague, butcher, linkboy of Cataline, lump of carrion, drunken fool, inhuman lunatic, feces, epicurean pig, assassin, temple robber, plunderer of Macedonia, infuriated pirate egged on by desire for booty and rapine...And yet it must be said that compared to Piso, Cataline was a Red Pepper."

This was followed by an expectant pause. Arthur leaned over the podium, gaped at his audience, and waited.

Someone whispered loudly—it may have been Aunt Haddy—Does he have to keep making those awful lists?

Arthur said it again: "Cataline was Red Pepper!"

Arthur's pasty face, his eyes imploring. Sarah nudged Walt: What's he talking about?

Shhhhhhhhhh.

Walt dug his mouth in his wife's ear. *Claude Pepper, the pinko senator. I think he's making a joke.* And so it was Walt who finally, out of mercy, rescued his brother by laughing. Everybody else followed his lead. Ah, Red Pepper! Cataline was a Red Pepper! Ha, ha. Ha.

Are you finished with this speech, Arthur?

One night, about a month or so later, it was Walt who after dinner took the book off the shelf in the living room where Sarah had safely stored it for posterity. He carried it upstairs to his study in the flat of his hand like a waiter carrying a tray. Then he locked the door and went to Rome. Night was thinning into morning by the time Cataline uttered the last of his famous last words: *But if fortune frowns on your bravery, take care not to die unavenged. Do not be captured and slaughtered like cattle, but, fighting like heroes, leave the enemy a bloody and tearful victory.*

Walt hears trumpets.

If fortune frowns! Viva Cataline! Viva the traitor!

Furthermore, as my brother so cogently argues, no self-respecting republic should be without a little healthy rebellion. It keeps everybody honest, and with a blowhard like Cicero around, somebody had to draw a line across the Forum with his sword. Walt slides off his chair and onto the carpet. He stares at the ceiling. His study has always been a box that envelops him, protects him. There are days he mourns this room, wonders how it will go on without him when he's gone. Right now, the distance between himself on the floor and the ceiling is intolerable.

I'm lying in a grave on my own carpet. To think there are people who believe that, when it's all over, the angels sing and we float up higher and higher. They don't doubt. They believe. Before I put on my other sock, I've doubted an entire day. And my brother writes: "The great revolutionist was found far in advance of his slain foemen, still breathing lightly, and showing on Cataline's face the indomitable spirit that had animated him when alive."

The Roman Army carried his severed head back to the Eternal City in a basket.

Once, outside this very room, a jay rammed into the window. Then he backed up and flew into it again. Again. Again. Again, until he finally dropped into the dirt. They say only man is valiant enough to die for lost causes.

In the blue gray light, Walt Kaplan thinks, My people sleep.

My own brother, a man who has faith enough—believes enough—to devote his life to raising an ancient debaucher from the dead, sleeps in leafy Brooklyn beside his squirrelly wife. My Sarah and my daughter sleep across the hall. In sleep, they breathe their finite breaths. The dawn sun claws upward. I sink into carpet. I dream of home when I'm home, of love when I love. How can I shout farewell from the mountaintop if I never leave the house? How, Arthur, can I rise to protect my people if I don't even own a sword?

FROM THE COLLECTED STORIES OF EDMUND JERRY (E. J.) HAHN, VOL. IV

*Somestories you drag around like old love and then something
reminds you, it could be anything, this half-empty mustard.*

—E. J. HAHN AT ANCHOR BAR, SUPERIOR, WISCONSIN

And still the dead they talk. Will they ever stop? E. J.
Hahn, my old boss, gone now more than a decade and
today he's back whispering in my ear about his yellow-and-
purple-daisied '69 VW bus, about piling in fourteen friends,
acquaintances, and a few folks he never laid eyes on before and
driving from Sheboygan to New York to see Joan Baez at the
Fillmore East. *Motherfucking Manhattan, I'm telling you.* From our
little cow-shit college in Wisconsin it was like landing on a ring
of Saturn. We didn't know our mothers' names. I don't remember a thing about the ride except the fog. Outside the can and
inside the van. E.J. nudging me. Nirvana highway, brother,
Heh, heh. And that Carrington drove through Ohio with his
feet. Tried it in Pennsylvania with his dick till he drove us off
the road. Carrington with a name like some Earl of Edinburgh,
though his parents were Christian Scientists from Rhinelander
County. Carrington, Carrington, Carrington. Whose idea it

was to buy the refrigerator for Chuck and Kathy D.? I told you about the refrigerator? About Chuck and Kathy D.? How they got married sophomore year and were so poor they couldn't afford to rent a place with a fridge, so to keep food from spoiling, Chuck would leave meat and sausages and cheese and eggs outside on the porch all night and then run out there at dawn, naked, grab the stuff, and throw it in a pan on the hot plate for breakfast, then nosedive back into their single little-boy bed and make fast and furious morning love to Kathy D. Oh, Kathy D.! One day Carrington and I were shoplifting in Sears and we saw this Frigidaire on sale for sixty-five dollars, and Carrington goes up to it and starts licking it, saying, My dearest, my dearest, till the salesman came over and said, What in holy name? And so we borrowed ten bucks from the salesman, who only wanted us lost, another seven from a woman in the sewing machine department, a five spot from the stock boy, another couple from a little old lady clutching her handbag in Housewares. We made the down payment. This was in '74 and we were Sheboygan's hippies. So unique in town we were almost a source of pride. Oh, Sheboygan: city of cheese curd and churches. The rest we got on credit. That fridge is still unpaid for, wherever it is, rusting away in oblivion. Our accounts will never balance. Of course, the problem with Carrington was he never stopped. The best hustlers can't. It was always something else. He started eight different folk bands our senior year, founded a commune on his cousin's farm in Oshkosh, asked for handouts, saying it's not a cult, it's about love, brothers and sisters, love. By then he was using heavier than the rest of us. Heroin got him bad in '76. The year of Our Lord, the Bicentennial. Jimmy Carter's buckteeth and Alfred

Joseph Carrington the Fourth on a float in the Fourth of July parade. God knows how he got up there, but there was Carrington, strung out in General Washington's boat crossing the Delaware, Cub Scouts dressed like elves straddling his legs and whacking him with paper muskets like he was some favorite drunken uncle.

He vanished for good the day after graduation. Not that he graduated. But he did dance across the stage wearing the empty diploma case on his head like a teepee. In '82 I got a letter from his lawyer brother. Carrington dead in Houston, a broken needle jammed in his arm. Our Duke of Cornwall bled to death in a motel room shower. The lawyer wrote. His death was a blessing, not very disguised. Can you beat that? His own brother. You run out of time is what I'm saying, is what I'm always saying. Whether you waste it or not. Some people you never shake. Carrington, what, dead fifteen years now and still he's egging me on? We dumped the fridge in the yard in front of Chuck and Kathy D.'s, and we'd crammed it full of Schlitz and watermelons. And Carrington, the maestro in a tux, and Kathy D. running barefoot across the snow, wide mouth, shocked, tits bobbing, yelling, Oh my gods! like she'd just won a convertible on *The Price Is Right,* except we were in Sheboygan, Wisconsin, my friend, and it was February and we were doing the hula around that sacred appliance in the snow, and oh how fucked up, oh how gloriously — never again — fucked up we were.

ACKNOWLEDGMENTS

The author wishes to express his gratitude to the editors of the below publications, for continuing to fight the good fight and publish stories. Stories in this collection first appeared, often in a different form, in: "Foley's Pond" and "The Vac-Haul" in *The Paris Review;* "Last Car Over the Sagamore Bridge" in *Harvard Review;* "Pampkin's Lament" in *McSweeney's;* "Occidental Hotel" and "The Divorce" in *Narrative;* "At the Kitchen Table" and "Dyke Bridge" in *Granta;* "Detamble," "Longfellow," "1979" in *Zyzzyva;* "From the Collected Stories of Edmund Jerry (E. J.) Hahn, Vol. IV" in 14 *Hills;* "Horace and Josephine" in 9*th Letter;* "Nathan Leopold Writes" in *Chicago Noir* (Akashic Books); "Herb and Rosalie Swanson at the Cocoanut Grove" in *Black Warrior Review* and *Bomb;* "Spokane" in *Bomb;* "Grand Pacific Hotel, Chicago, 1875" in *Ploughshares;* "Plaza Revolución, Mexico City, 6 a.m." in *Witness;* "Waldheim" in *New American Writing;* "Reverend Hrncirik Receives an Airmail Package" in *The Southern Review;* "Lubyanka Prison, Moscow, 1940" (as "Babel") in *Cutbank;* "Denny Coughlin: In Memory" in *Grantland;* "Woman in a Dubrovnik Café" in *The Cincinnati Review;* "Roman Morning" in *Mississippi Review;*

"Renters" in *World Literature Today;* "Eisendrath (as "No Light"), "Paddy Bauler in a Quiet Moment," "The Mayor's Dream" (as "Mayor Daley's Dream"), and "Harold Washington Walks at Midnight" in *A Public Space;* "February 26, 1995" in *Guernica;* "Geraldo, 1986" and "Shhhhhh, Arthur's Studying" in *Conjunctions;* "Belief, 1999" in *The Return of Král Majáles* (Litteraria Pragensia Books / Charles University, Czech Republic); "On the 14" (as "On the 88") in the *San Francisco Chronicle;* "Waukegan Story" in *Third Coast;* "The Moors of Chicago" in *Once.* "Pampkin's Lament" was reprinted in the *Pushcart Prize Anthology XXXII.*

The line at the end of "The Poet" is from William Meredith's "The Wreck of the Thresher (Lost at Sea, April 10, 1963)."

[Further acknowledgements TK]

ABOUT THE AUTHOR

PETER ORNER was born in Chicago and is the author of three acclaimed books, *Esther Stories, The Second Coming of Mavala Shikongo,* and *Love and Shame and Love.* Orner is also the editor of two books of nonfiction, *Underground America* and *Hope Deferred: Narratives of Zimbabwean Lives.* His work has appeared in *The Best American Short Stories, The Atlantic,* the *New York Times,* and *The Paris Review* and has been awarded two Pushcart Prizes. A 2006 Guggenheim Fellow, Orner teaches at San Francisco State University. He lives in San Francisco.